Trespassing

Other Titles by Debby Topliff

And the Word Became Color
Painting Revelation DVD
She Belongs to Me
Squirrel Tales
Hiding

Trespassing

a novel

Debby Topliff

Published by Firefly Life
730 North Maple Street
Saugatuck, Michigan 49453

ISBN: 978-0-9975889-0-3 (softcover)
ISBN: 978-0-9975889-1-0 (ebook)

Cover art and design: Todd T. Norman
Interior design: Beth Shagene

Printed in the United States of America
2016 — First edition

To Nana—
who loved houses and gardens and me

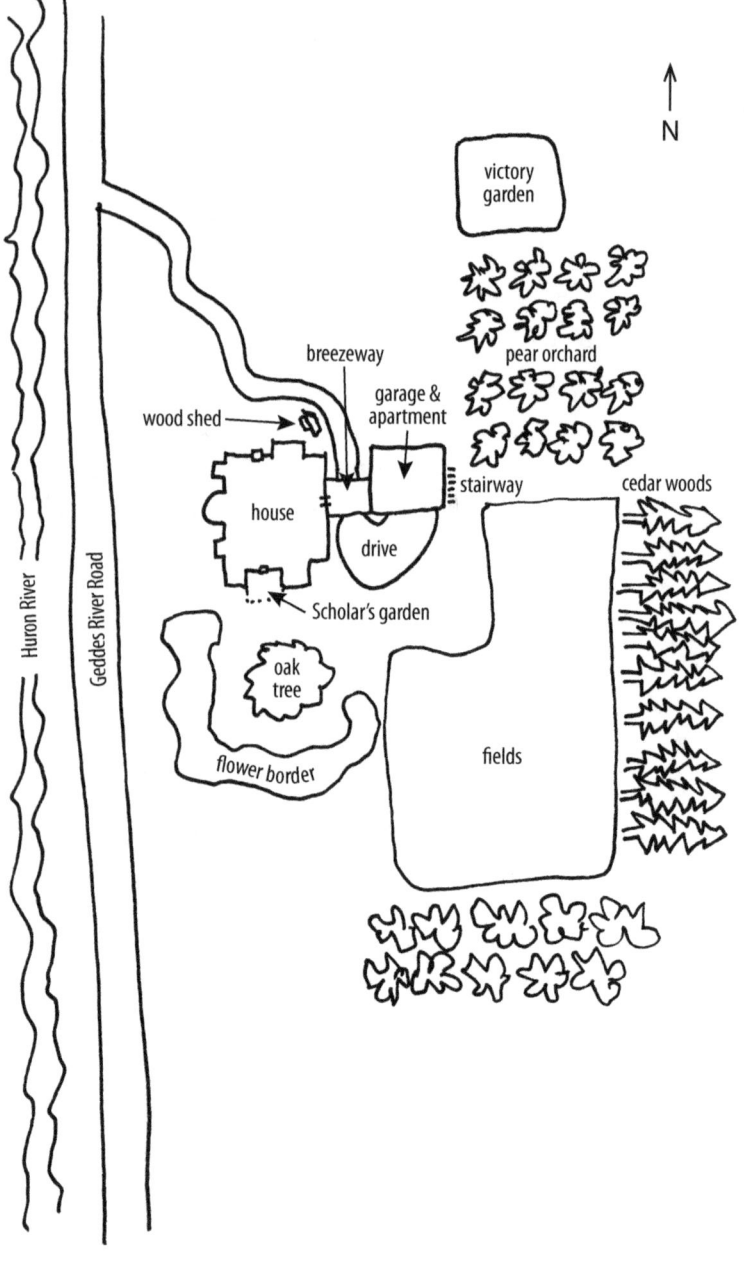

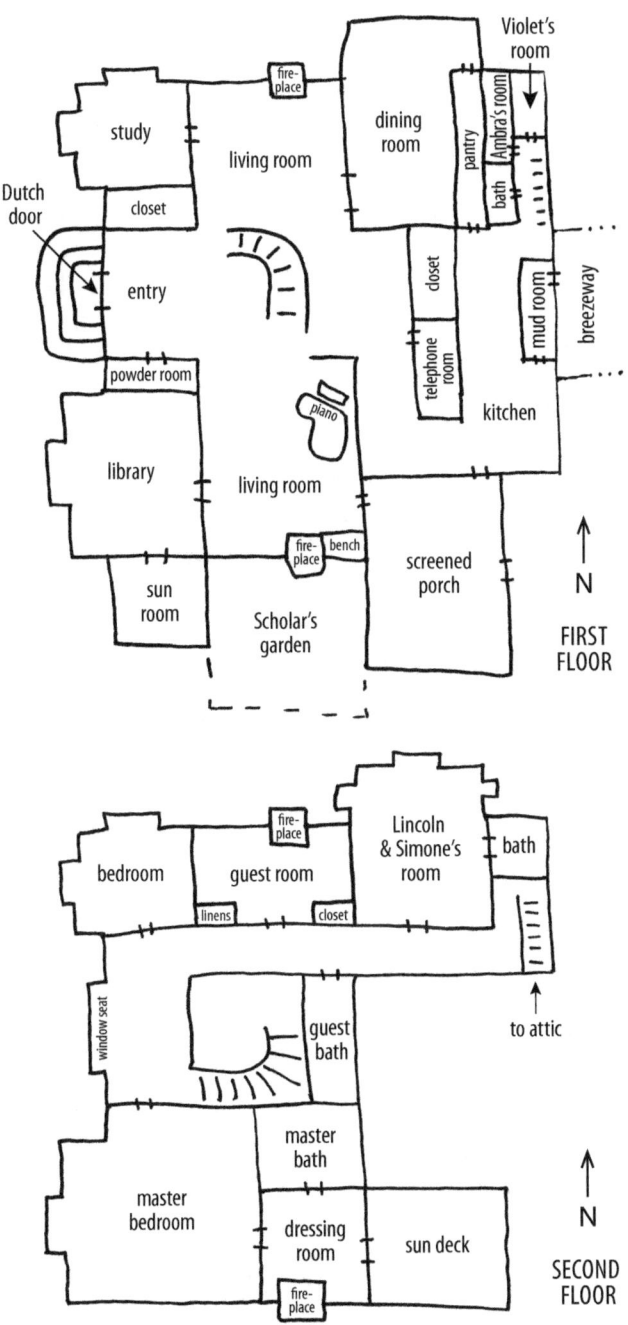

The house movers had never tackled such a project.
Clearly the house would first need to be divided.

Chapter 1

THE OLD FARMHOUSE WAS BIG. Big enough to be two
fine houses and a roomy bungalow. In fact that's what
happened shortly after this story took place. Mrs. Lincoln
Blankwell, Sr. opened her copy of the *Michigan Daily* in the
spring of 1947 and read that the United States Government
was going to build a Veteran's Hospital smack on top of the
prettiest piece of property east of the Huron River.

Despite Mrs. Blankwell, Sr.'s numerous angry protests to
the impudent people at the Office of Veterans' Affairs, the
property was taken from them under the right of eminent
domain. By summer the old farmhouse was bisected right
through the middle, roof and all. The attached garage was
amputated like a gangrenous limb. Then the two halves of
the house, domestic Siamese twins, were lifted on a squad-
ron of dollies and rolled down the road to where they still
stand today. The former grand front door with its colon-
nades and circular steps now looks directly across a sprout
of lawn and into what once was its own less majestic, yet

respectable back porch. The garage, big enough itself for three cars, a tractor mower, and the handyman apartment upstairs, must have been hauled off in another direction and camouflaged behind flower boxes, for no one knows its whereabouts today.

In the middle of March that year, a mighty wind left over from winter catapulted the arctic air crouching up in Canada, hurled it over the northern Great Lakes, across pine forests, through open fields, down the Huron River valley, and dumped it thick and wet on that big old farmhouse in Ann Arbor, Michigan.

At that very hour Violet Thomas, the Blankwell's new maid, stopped at the top of the big front stairs to rest for a while on the window seat. She loved being the only one home. She had worked all day dusting, mopping floors, plumping feather cushions, wiping smudges from the woodwork. Now, as she peered out over the western sky, thick flakes of snow swarmed and roosted on the winter-brown lawn. The storm brooded like a dark army camouflaged in white.

Violet stood and smoothed out the wrinkles on the front of her uniform. Only one more task before dinner—to straighten Simone's room before she got back from her watercolor class at the fancy Women's City Club downtown. Miss Simone was the Blankwell's daughter-in-law, Mr. Lincoln junior's showy new bride. Though Violet felt twice her age, they were both twenty and both recently transplanted from the South. Lincoln was off to Chicago for a few days on one of his business trips. His parents, the Blankwell seniors, were doing their post-war duty of helping the European economy and wintering in the south of France. Their steamer wouldn't set sail from Naples for New York until the daffodils, whose heads were just now poking out of the cold Michigan clay, had opened their petticoats to dance in the April sun.

And then there was Randolph. Violet paused at the thought of him. He was giving piano lessons at Liberty Music near campus like he did every afternoon. He was studying classical music at the University as a graduate student on the G.I. Bill and earning room and board as handyman to the Blankwells, though he would bristle at the label. He said he only stooped to chop wood and shovel walks as a temporary concession on his way to concert hall fame. He had said yes to Mrs. Blankwell's ad for room and board when she threw in a practice piano—and after he spotted the two young women residents, ivory and ebony, one at the at front door, one at the back.

Violet rested her hand lightly on the knob to Simone's door. Why were her fingers trembling? Her mother's voice sang in her head. "Child," she had said as Violet boarded the northbound train in Missouri, "abide in the Lord and his fruit will abide in you." Violet had nodded at her mother but her heart tugged in two directions. She hated to leave her home and family, yet adventure lay before her like a silver fork in the road. "And honey," her mother had added as the train jerked forward. "Don't forget self-control. It tastes bitter at first, but later yields the peaceful fruit of righteousness to those who are trained by it."

Her mother's words clung to her like the scent of pine bark back home, but she shook her head and gave a quick look down the hall, seized the handle to Simone's door, and stepped into the room.

It was a mess as usual, with the stench of cigarette smoke everywhere. Even Lincoln's bed, though unslept in since he was away on his trip, was littered with Simone's cast off clothing. All the bedrooms in this big house had twin beds. Didn't white folk sleep together?

Simone's sheets were twisted in a knot. Her silky night-gown and matching robe lay rumpled on the floor. Did the girl ever sleep? Lord knows she spent enough time in her room. The heavy glass ashtray on the side table was full of cigarette butts, Chesterfields nicked with red. How could Lincoln stand such a filthy habit? Violet gathered the dirty laundry into a bundle by the door. Then she picked up the gown and robe and laid them open on Lincoln's bed. Tiny blue forget-me-nots bloomed over the pale green skirt and down the placket of the robe, like spring back home in Missouri.

She hesitated just a moment, then quickly slipped off her blue uniform with its stiff white collar and draped it over a chair. She unhooked her bra and slid the silky gown over her head, adjusting the straps and smoothing the lace bodice across her breasts. Perfect. She and Simone were nearly mirror images of one another in shape and size. And their great, great, great grandmothers had both departed from the same longitude in the summer of 1754 to cross the Atlantic. But Simone's set sail from Southampton, England, snuggled inside a tall coil of rope on the sunny deck of the Independence where she sang songs to her porcelain-headed doll. Violet's, on the other hand, had a different relationship with ropes, captive in a dark holding bay of an unnamed ship that left during the night from Sierra Leone.

Violet put on the robe and held out her arms, twisting and swaying like a spring willow in the wind. The fabric whispered against her skin. She tried to see herself in the full-length mirror, but the room was too dark for a good look, so she went to the big window and pulled back the heavy drapes, coaxing in what was left of the snowy afternoon light. She climbed onto the bay window seat, careful not to step on the gown's lacy hem, and looked west. The cold air felt wonderful on her work-warmed skin. She pressed her cheek against the pane. From here she could just make out the bend in the river and the tall shape of the Bell Tower on its far side, marking the edge of the University. Not that she'd been on campus more than two or three times. Once to get her teeth cleaned; Mrs. Blankwell insisted on that. And once to see a movie with a girl who worked down the road. On her afternoons off she preferred the company of fox squirrels and the occasional otter over in the woods by the river. She was looking forward to spring. But the tree branches were again heavy with snow and the long winding driveway up to the house looked like a frozen river.

Up to now, snow had been her greatest delight in living in the north. The little snow they got in southern Missouri melted when it touched the ground. She had been unprepared for just how white and pure those frozen bits of water could be, like tiny stars dropped from heaven to cover the earth. *Though your sins be as scarlet, they shall be whiter than snow.* Her mother's voice again. It had been early November when she first saw snow. Ambra the cook was clanking in the kitchen, making Saturday pancakes. Randolph was outside her window chopping wood. But the sound of the ax was muted; the natural world felt quiet and far away. When she peeked past her curtain she saw that the setting moon was still bright. The whole yard, the woodshed, the hedge of squared-off boxwood, the thick carpet of myrtle trailing round to the side of the porch— everything looked like it was covered with Mama's birth-day frosting.

Why didn't she welcome snow today? She gazed out the window. The northern regiment of clouds had advanced across the river and was marching toward town, lining up like enemy soldiers before a strike. She looked down at the gown she was wearing; the white lace rested on her dark breasts like snowflakes on cedar. She put her hands on her hips and arched her back like she'd seen Simone do when she thought no one was watching. Simone, the great actress. She wore a smile in the main part of the house, but Violet heard the afternoons of crying and the late-night whimpers through the floor above her room after Lincoln's moan became a snore.

The table lamp gave off just enough light so Violet could see her reflection in the window. She tilted her head side to side, turned, and looked at herself from behind. What would Lincoln think if he saw *her* wrapped in Simone's icy silk? Would he want to stretch his white fingers around her waist, encircling her like he did Simone? She laughed and raised a finger, pointing at herself in the window: *You shouldn't be thinking of Mr. Lincoln like that.*

Suddenly she gasped. A truck was pulling up the drive, Randolph's truck. She grabbed the edge of the drape and twisted behind it, her heart racing. Had he seen her? Would he tell? She waited until his taillights passed under the breezeway between the house and garage, then jumped down from the window seat.

As she did, something fell to the floor: three small watercolors the size of postcards that must have been propped up behind the curtain. One was a picture of the giant oak in the middle of the back yard, the one with the love seat built around its thick trunk. Another showed a long view to the river with a cardinal against a grey sky. The third, the one she couldn't stop looking at, was a picture of her. A tawny-skinned woman dressed in a blue uniform was standing in what had to be the library downstairs, hands reaching forward, head tilted to the side, facing a large globe.

Violet blushed. Simone had been spying on her yesterday. The house had so many nooks and crannies she could have been hiding anywhere. No wonder Randolph called Simone cat-girl and said she was as dangerous as the leopard whose fur she wore. Had she been watching yesterday when Violet was dusting knickknacks on the living room mantle? Randolph had brought in wood to lay a fire. He had suddenly grabbed hold of her ankle with his strong piano-playing fingers. She froze. He leaned close... She kicked him away and shook her feather duster in his ruddy face. He coughed and let go, but stood up slowly, tracing the line of her calf with the tip of his bushy red mustache. "Mighty fine," he whispered in her ear. She shushed him and told him he was an old bear who should still be in hibernation. "In my lair?" he laughed as he left the room. She ducked into the library and stood next to the globe, spinning it fast, letting her fingers glide over the smooth blue of the oceans, wishing, hoping, even praying she could find a way around trouble.

Yet now she was dressed in trouble. She threw off the robe and peeled the gown over her head. She fumbled back into her clothes, jabbing at buttons and listening for any sound of a door opening downstairs. She checked the clock between the twin beds. Nearly four-thirty. Randolph was early. Maybe the storm had forced him home. Maybe Simone would cut short her afternoon too. Quickly she made up the one slept-in bed, hung the robe and gown on a hook in the closet, and hurried downstairs to finish dinner preparations for Miss Simone.

Chapter 2

Simone shut the heavy Dutch door and hung her wet coat over the bench in the front entryway. She flicked melting snow from her tangle of shoulder-length hair and stepped out of her wet loafers. She'd had to walk to the house from the bottom of the drive and now there were oxblood stains on her white bobby socks. But who cares, she thought. No one was home to notice or scold. The Gestapo was gone.

She was glad her friend had been driving. The storm had come out of nowhere, as if the world had been turned upside down and shaken like a snow globe. She wouldn't have been able to maneuver the long driveway in her mother-in-law's Studebaker. Driving on snow still frightened her. Lincoln had tried to give her a lesson one Sunday in November after the first big snowfall. He'd taken her to an empty lot and made her drive his swanky little BMW fast until it spun out of control.

"No," he'd shouted when she slid the car into a row of

arborvitae on the edge of the lot. "You've got to turn the wheel the other way."

"But that's where I *don't* want to go."

"It's a law of physics, Simone." There was more than impatience in Lincoln's voice. "Two opposing vectors added together create a new direction."

"Stop flaunting your fancy education." He always made her feel so stupid. During their courtship, he sent her letters back with the misspellings corrected in red.

"It's not my fault you didn't finish school," he said getting out of the passenger seat so he could drive home.

"You're the one who asked me to marry you," she said over the glimmer of the silver roof. He walked around the front; she walked around the back.

"And you're the one who said yes." They slammed their doors in unison.

"I said yes to marriage, not to some course in physics—or grammar."

"I've already explained about that," he said. "I just can't understand why you don't want to improve yourself, why you don't care about doing things the right way."

"You mean your way."

"No, I mean the right way. The square root of sixty-four is always eight. That's not something I made up."

"And the square root of marriage?" she asked. "What would that be? Two opposing personalities arguing until they move in different directions?" She wasn't so dumb. But it gave her a headache to analyze things. She'd rather thumb through one of her art history books or stare out the window at shape and color than talk about how a combustion engine worked or why they had to get rid of Harry

Truman. Most of all she'd rather drift off at the piano in Beethoven's "Moonlight Sonata."

She balanced her shoes upside down on the radiator. Lincoln—or his mother—would tell her to stuff newspaper in the toes, but they weren't here. She'd like a new pair of loafers, anyway. She'd seen some in a window downtown, with gold buckles across the top, like tiny horses' bits. Those would look nice with knee socks and her red kilt with its gold kilt pin. Lincoln wouldn't mind. He liked dressing her up.

Sounds and smells of cooking came from the kitchen. Fried chicken tonight. She glanced at the grandfather clock in the hall as she went into the study and dropped her portfolio and paint supplies on the chintz sofa. Just past four-thirty. Dinner wasn't until seven—or could things change now that she was the only one home? Did she have to eat in the dining room all by herself? Last night she'd had a terrible headache and Violet brought her a boiled egg in her room. Then she'd fallen asleep and missed Lincoln's call. It was odd to be alone with none of the family here, just the help. Even Ambra had been given three days off while Lincoln was out of town. She had begged him to take her along. What was she supposed to do for three days without him? But No, he said, it was just business. He'd be with clients all day, and then have to take them to dinner at night. She'd be bored stiff. Well, she was bored stiff now.

Chapter 3

RANDOLPH STAMPED SNOW from his boots and brushed it from the top of his head. He should have worn his hat. The first flakes had begun only half an hour ago and already more than an inch had accumulated on the outside stairs to his rooms above the garage. The music store sent him home early. The radio said they were in for a blizzard. Good thing he'd put his truck in the garage, in Lincoln's stall. Simone must have gotten back early, too. He'd seen fresh footprints leading up the drive to the front door. He jiggled the door handle and nudged with his knee, then ducked to enter the low opening into his rooms above the garage. "Damn," he said as his glasses steamed up. Michigan weather was as fickle as a woman. Spring posed and flirted, lifted her skirt, blew in your ear, then turned a cold shoulder and howled at you with freezing wind. He hung his plaid jacket on a hook and bent down to unlace his boots. Melting snow dripped from the ends of his thick red mustache.

He winced as he tugged on the leather laces and let

go with another curse. His left thumb throbbed. He'd smashed it when he'd been straightening out the wood-pile. That would set him back a day or more on his practice schedule. He put the tender thumb in his mouth. Why had he ever agreed to this manual labor, chopping and stacking and carrying wood? His fingers were his life. They were his paintbrush on the canvas of keys. He couldn't afford damage of any kind. They were his soldiers in the field, a highly trained battalion, marching in formation, each one doing exactly as he commanded. Now he had become one of Mrs. B's enlisted men. When she spoke he had to hup two, stack the wood, then hit the right keys and make a sweet sound. Yes Ma'am.

He didn't mind Yes Ma'am and Yes Sir; they were just necessary steps on his way up and out and on to the top. Yes Ma'am to Harriet, Mrs. Blankwell-the-elder. And yes Ma'am to Simone, the brand new Mrs. Blankwell, even though she was barely out of her teens. Then Yes Sir to the old man and his silver-spoon son. But not to Violet; he called her by name.

Violet. He lined up his boots on the mat under the narrow bench by the door and walked, sock footed, over to the love seat next to the space heater that warmed his two small rooms. He sat down and pulled out the tails of his shirt to wipe the condensation off his glasses. Violet. He tilted the glasses until he could see his own reflection, tiny in the curved lens. He didn't look so bad, though his hair was thinning on top, receding over his temples. What had Violet called him yesterday? A burly, brown bear come too soon from his lair? That girl amazed him, so quiet and calm behind her grey-brown eyes, soft as rabbit fur. Her words, so few and far between, sounded like poetry. She couldn't have had much schooling. She was just a maid, helping in the kitchen, cleaning the house, making the beds. He held that image and let his mind drift over her dark caramel skin. Her fingertips smoothing clean cotton sheets, her strong hands pulling tight the wool blankets. He pictured her fluffing the feather pillows, clutching them under her chin, against her breast. He wondered if a trace of her scent lingered on the pillowcases. He wanted to know that smell. If he was a bear, then she was honey, dark golden honey.

He looked at his watch: twenty to five. He'd have an hour or more at the old upright in the corner to work on that arpeggio that was tripping him up. That's why he was here, really. That's why he lowered himself to become a handyman for this family of peacocks. It wasn't the free room and board, though that helped. It was the old piano that Mrs. B had used as bait to hook him. She had talked some friends of hers out of their scratched up Baldwin, and then she'd hired two men with a winch truck to hoist the piano up from the garage parking lot below. He could hardly believe the tenacity of that woman. He had to give her credit: what Mrs. Blankwell wanted Mrs. Blankwell got. Well mostly. Randolph had a strong suspicion that Simone had not been part of her plan. Such a young, inexperienced girl for old Lincoln, the Blankwell's number one heir. Not only was she a southerner, but a Catholic one at that. Back in his home in New Orleans, she'd have been a plum. But not here, not in the cold Protestant North.

"I know you professional pianists practice hours and hours a day," Mrs. B had told him. "Having a piano of your own means you can do your scales—or whatever it is you do—morning, noon, and night without disturbing anyone. All I ask is that maybe, once or twice, you'd do me the great honor of playing a few pieces in the house, when I host the bridge group or the Garden Club?" She posed it as a question, but Randolph knew better. "I'll pay you, of course." Mrs. Blankwell was sly as well as determined. He didn't miss the message behind her words: the Steinway Grand in their living room was off limits except at her request.

He snagged an edge of the piano stool with one foot, rolled it over, and sat down. He knew he wasn't a traditionally handsome man. A squarish head and a shrug to his shoulders made him look stiff and uncomfortable when he stood or walked. But when he sat in front of the keyboard, that shrug became a royal cape. His hands elegance. Music power.

He settled the stool in place, then spread his arms winglike and flew up and down the keys, circling the energy captured in the space between his chest and arms, drawing the vibrations into a harmonious ball of sound. His hands were gentle claws hovering above the keys like a mother eagle landing on her nest. His thighs, planted firm in front of him, rose with just the slightest lift as he pumped the pedals. He tipped his head to the left and floated on the deep resonance of the bass notes. He banked to the right, riding the frothy high currents. Sometimes he hung his head over the keys, over his hands, as if he was hunting for prey, searching for some deep truth between the black and white beneath his fingers.

When he finished he sat up straight with his face lifted to the ceiling, waiting for the ghost of the music he had stirred and driven from the strings to descend upon him like a dove.

Then he stood and walked over to the sink in the corner of the sitting room and turned on the hot water. Carefully he unhooked his glasses from his ears and set them on a shelf. He pulled off his wool sweater and draped it over the back of a chair, unbuttoned his shirt, and stripped down to his hairy chest. The silver ankh he wore on a chain glimmered through his auburn curls. The small purple scar on his left rib cage where a German bullet had grazed his side was barely visible. He lathered his hands with soap and started to wash. He wanted to be clean, to smell like Ivory, when he sat down at the kitchen table with Violet.

Moving a house is an art handed down from one generation to another. In fact, since the mid 1800s, any house, cottage, garage, or pole barn in the southeastern corner of Michigan finding itself in a new location has been hauled there by members of one family.

Chapter 4

THE FIRST TIME VIOLET CAUGHT SIGHT of the old farmhouse she had been sitting in the big backseat of Mrs. Blankwell's Studebaker. The Blankwell's didn't have a chauffeur like most of their friends, but Mrs. Blankwell didn't mind, in fact she relished every opportunity to drive the car, imagining herself at the helm of her own personal battleship. That day in early June she picked Violet up at the Ann Arbor train station, then drove over a bridge and along the river, turning up a long gravel drive that wound past an orchard of trees loaded with blossoms. Beyond the orchard a wide, golden-green field ended at a dark cedar woods. Off to one side of the rolling lawn, far from the house, lay a naked patch of crusty earth with a scarecrow posted at its center.

"Our victory garden," Mrs. Blankwell said. "We certainly did what we could to help win that war."

The house sat at the top of the hill like a wedding cake waiting for guests to arrive. Shiny wide windows gleamed in the sun, framed with green shutters against white clapboard siding. The roof perched like a jaunty red hat, peaks every which way, with two cobblestone chimneys pinning it down.

Mrs. Blankwell drove under a breezeway that led to a long garage, then circled and pulled up to a door at the back of the house. "We'll get out here," she said, looking back at Violet. "You can bring in the luggage later." She sprang from the driver's seat, a tiny woman, yet strong as steel. She reached her arms calisthenically above her head, stretched side to side, and then strode into the house.

Violet grabbed her satchel and followed.

"This is the mudroom," Mrs. Blankwell said over her shoulder. "The porch is through there. This, of course, is the kitchen."

Violet tried to take it all in. What was a mudroom? Was that large stainless steel cabinet with two doors the refrigerator?

"The pantry leads to the dining room. That door goes to the cellar, this one to the back stairs. And here, past Ambra's room—she's the cook—and the back bath, is *your* room." Mrs. Blankwell strode through the door and pulled the chain on the shaded bulb in the center of the ceiling.

The tiny room glowed mossy green, like a secret clearing in the middle of a thicket. Her own room. Joy bubbled up in Violet's chest and she wanted to throw up her hands and say *Hallelujah*, but she kept her lips pressed, her eyes straight. She knew her place. She was the hired help.

Chapter 5

Simone turned her satchel upside down and emptied her paints and brushes onto the sofa in the cozy study. No need to tidy up yet. Lincoln wouldn't be back until Friday. She could spread herself out, make a mess, do whatever she wanted. She unzipped her portfolio and took out the block of watercolor pages and stuck her thumbnail under the top piece, splitting off the picture she'd worked on in class.

The snow was coming down hard now, forming a lacy curtain on the outside of the window. Maybe tomorrow she'd go out and make snow angels. Too bad there was no one to play with. She took the roll of masking tape from her bag and taped the watercolor—a still life of blue and green bottles on a yellow tablecloth—onto the big surface on the side of the windowsill. The windowsills were the best part of the house. She loved to sit on them with her knees under her chin and stare out, away from this foreign family, away from all the dos and don'ts, away from the tiny room within her that sometimes roared liked a furnace, sometimes burned cold like dry ice.

There were extra deep windowsills in all the rooms except maybe the kitchen. She wasn't sure about the kitchen. She didn't feel comfortable going in there. Mrs. Blankwell—she couldn't make herself call her mother-in-law Harriet—told her, "Let the help help." So when she wanted something, she pulled one of the corded ropes that connected to a set of buzzers in the kitchen and Ambra would come to whatever room she was in and take her request. Ambra would bring her breakfast in bed or a snack in the sunroom. On cold afternoons like this one, especially if her in-laws were out, she'd ask for tea or hot cocoa in the study and Ambra would bring it along with fresh-baked cookies or a piece of chocolate cake. Ambra was always trying to fatten her up.

Ambra reminded her of home, her real home. She talked in watery sentences that rolled and meandered and never seemed to end, just like the Mississippi. Flecks of silver hair tinged the edges of her face like a tiny tiara. The wide shelf of her bosom curved in just slightly above the wider expanse of her belly. Her hands were large and strong, her knuckles thick. She had a deep mannish voice, but Ambra was the most motherly woman Simone had ever known.

On dark winter mornings when Simone didn't show up for breakfast—Lincoln left for work before she was awake and she hated to sit with her in-laws—Ambra would bring her a tray with juice and coffee and a poached egg with honey-butter biscuits. She'd set it beside the girl, shining love at Simone with her doey eyes.

Just yesterday Simone was hiding in her bathroom when she heard Ambra's heavy footsteps climbing the back stairs.

"Miss Simone," she said tapping against the door. Simone heard Ambra step into the room and gasp. "You all right, child? You need my help?" Then there was a gasp and Simone knew Ambra must have seen the thick smear, dark as crude oil, trailing from the center of her bed to its edge.

"I'm fine. It's just my time of the month."

"From the looks of things, I suspect it be more than that, Miss Simone," Ambra said through the door. "You got aching in your belly?"

Simone quickly flushed away the bloody mess and washed her hands.

"I'm fine," she said again, opening the door. "If you can just take care of those sheets for me…" She walked over to the chaise and sank down. "I'm afraid I've made an awful mess."

"Of course, Missy. I'll tend to them."

"And hand me my Chesterfields. Over there by the bed."

Ambra made a clucking sound under her breath. "It may not be my place to say it, but Lord knows I've come to care for you. And a soul can't help but read the signs right before her eyes, what with every one of us living here under the same roof. So I'm going to speak my mind." She unfolded her hands from on top of her belly where they had been resting and pointed a finger. "If you're planning on being a mother, Miss Simone, you must treat your body like the temple God intended."

The body a temple? Simone hadn't heard that one

before. She thought of the tiny knots of flesh that kept ripping their way out of her. Maybe that's why the church at home insisted on baptizing babies. Her hands shook as she lit a cigarette and took a drag. "Heavens, Ambra." She exhaled a long plume of smoke. "I've only been married half a year. I'm hardly past the honeymoon stage." She pulled her robe closer. "Would you bring me that eiderdown?" Suddenly she felt shivery. Ice cold. If she couldn't manage to become a mother, then what in the world was she going to be? She had to show Lincoln—and his mother—that she could produce something.

Ambra spread the down comforter over Simone's thin frame. "I'll make you my healing broth before I leave, and bring it up for an early lunch. That'll put some blood back in your veins." She crossed to the door and looked back. "You listen now, Miss Simone. Any more bleeding and you tell me. Right away. No one else has to know. I don't want you slipping away like some snagged log pulled under by the current. You hear?"

"I do."

"I'm off to Detroit until Saturday to help my daughter with her new baby, but I'll tell Violet to take good care of you."

"Do you have to go?" Simone nearly cried.

"And one more thing." Ambra paused until Simone looked up. "You keep Mr. Lincoln in his own bed. At least for a week. It's a good thing he's gone out of town for a few days." She turned and shut the door quietly.

A week? She sucked at her cigarette. Lincoln didn't cater to the church's view that sex was only for procreation.

Keeping him out of her bed would be like telling him to leave his precious car in the garage.

And now the garage was empty. The house was empty. She was stuck here alone, tired and hungry. She'd like a pot of tea, but Ambra was gone. She felt odd knowing it was only Violet out in the kitchen. Maybe Randolph was home early, too. Why should she be afraid of them? They were the help. She knew what Lincoln would say. He'd say, Grow up, Simone. Remember who you are. You are Mrs. Lincoln Blankwell, Jr. She reached for the thin cord hanging behind the sofa and gave it a tug.

Chapter 6

LINCOLN'S MARRIAGE TO SIMONE was a slap in his mother's face, a quick, clean way to snip the apron string once for all and drop old Harriet from around his neck. At an early age he'd trained himself to listen to his mother with only half an ear. He discovered the magic of saying "Yes Mum" to whatever idiotic demands she made. Yes Mum, I won't be late. Yes Mum, I won't forget. Yes Mum, I'll drive with utmost caution. His mother would smile and he'd go off to do whatever he wanted. Eighty, ninety, a hundred miles per hour in his 1938 BMW 328 Roadster. The car was one of only a handful in the United States. One of his well-connected fraternity brothers brought it over from Germany when the war ended. Lincoln gave it to himself as an early wedding present—a goodbye gift to the single life. For twenty-nine years he'd done as he pleased: New England prep school, Ivy League college, a few war years stateside at a desk in the Navy. Then he'd moved back home and joined his father's business.

His mother wouldn't let up her endless harangue on

marriage and what sort of woman was suitable for the family. What ancestral lineage, paternal occupation, private schooling, religious background. She prepped him on the subtle gradations of denominations: Anglican at the top, of course, then Presbyterian, Congregational, Methodist. There was something wrong with the Lutherans but he wasn't sure what. The bottom of the list hardly mattered, Baptists, Unitarians, Christian Scientists. They weren't even close to being acceptable. Heaven knows why. She had even given him a lecture on bone structure and well-spaced teeth. Dentists could drain your bank account, she said, faster than a rubber plug pulled from a tub of hot water.

His mother took it worse than he did when Virginia Needhouse, his childhood sweetheart, returned his engagement ring. She had fit his mother's bill to a tee—whatever that meant—and more so. But Ginny had her sights fixed higher than an old Ann Arbor family and when she snagged a fellow from Lake Forest, Lincoln had bowed out gracefully. He and Ginny had a good thing going. That needn't change.

His mother quickly recovered from the embarrassment of Ginny's rejection and made it more clear than ever that she expected him to marry a Daughter of the American Revolution from Miss Porter's and Wellesley whose father was not only president of the bank but head of the vestry at St. Whomever's Episcopal Church in Well Groomed City, USA. To his mother, USA meant any state north of the Mason Dixon Line that had gained its statehood before 1837. Even some of the original thirteen colonies didn't make that cut. But his mother had high moral principles to uphold. She was a founding member of the Ann Arbor chapter of Moral Rearmament and she looked askance at any state that had ever participated in the barbarous practice of slavery. She took it as one of her personal missions to rescue her share of Negroes from the South and give them a chance for true freedom at her house in the liberty-loving North. That's why all their help were colored and why she went to the extra trouble and expense to import them from the South.

But it wasn't completely true that all the help were Negroes. When their gardener and all-around handyman had suddenly gone off in August with a maid from down the road, his mother had made a radical departure and hired that odd brute from the University. Lincoln could tell he was a crafty fellow and not at all the sort who would know how to keep the Blankwells in fresh-cut flowers and blotch-less tomatoes. He was studying music, not horticulture, and going for a masters degree at that. Lincoln knew the type, working himself up in the world by mere brainpower, thinking himself refined just because he knew the classics. He wouldn't last long. Lincoln gave him until the dandelions went to seed.

But perhaps Randolph fit into his mother's missionary plan since he was from the south. You couldn't get much farther south than New Orleans. His mother had heard him playing the piano one afternoon during a luncheon at the Women's City Club. Or was it the Ann Arbor Lawn and Garden Club? All those women's things seemed the same to him. It was Simone's duty to keep that stuff sorted out, not his. Why would he want all that chitter-chatter filling up his mind? He knew what he liked. He knew what he wanted. And he was quite certain he knew how to get it: say what people wanted to hear, protect your reputation at all costs, and tend the web of influential acquaintances.

Meanwhile he was still living at home, still being fed with Ambra's first class cooking, still having his Brooks Brother's shirts hand washed and impeccably ironed by that spicy new girl, Violet. But to top it all off, he had a saucy young wife in his bedroom every night, a child, really, a skinny young thing with good bones. Old Harriet had to give him credit for that. But she was from Kentucky, had never been to college, and—the final blow—she was a Catholic. Or rather, she had been a Catholic. He knew there was no way his family, or he, himself, could stomach a Catholic wedding. He had heard they conducted the whole thing like a Mass, with those awful brittle wafer things daubed into a communal goblet shared by all the guests. But Simone hadn't put up a fight. Episcopal priests wore collars and robes just like the Catholic ones did. Who could tell the difference? What he didn't know was that Simone had been desperate for an excuse to keep the door open for divorce. So they ended up getting married in the back garden of her parents' house in Louisville. It wasn't like a church at all except for the inevitable prayers at the beginning and end and a brief stint on their knees during he wasn't sure what. Religion fit into the scheme of his life just a tad under the Woman's City Club. Come to think of it, wasn't church just the Women's City Club except inside stained glass windows and under a mansard roof?

It isn't often that house movers are called upon to cut a house in two. Most houses big enough for more than one family make peace with the land and send down permanent roots. Most houses big enough for two dwellings have plenty of rooms for warring parties to stake out their own territory, with neutral space in between.

Chapter 7

VIOLET HEARD THE BUZZ from the call box in the corner of the kitchen and looked up from the sink where she was peeling potatoes. It was from the study. Her highness was home. She'd just have to wait. Didn't Simone know Violet was busy cooking *her* dinner? Why couldn't she at least sashay her skinny little self to the kitchen and stick her royal face through the door and ask for tea? Of course she couldn't be expected to fill the kettle or light a burner. She might chip one of her perfect nails or splash water on her cashmere sweater. Violet made a mental note. She would try one of those sweaters on next time she was alone in Simone's room, perhaps the deep rose one with pearl buttons across one shoulder.

Rose. Rosie. Her sister. She missed that sweet, soft

flower of a girl who always had a smile for her, and a one-armed hug. She and Rosie were twins but they didn't look alike, not at all, not anymore than a violet looked like a rose. Violet was tall and willowy like Mama, sharp and to the point, with delicate features and a slender nose. Her words numbered few, like the petals of her name, but her thoughts plunged deep and strong as the dark purple blooms that peeked out from under the violet's heart-shaped leaves. She was the first born. "You came straight out," Mama always said, "with your fuzzy little head and your pixie face. Cute as a baby squirrel. Skin soft as velvet with a purple glow. My royal violet."

When Rosie followed, something went wrong. She was big and round. The cord came out first, pinched off the oxygen. The midwife worked hard, but part of Rosie's brain had already died. That's why she carried her head off to one side and her right arm withered. That's why a little drool seeped out the corner of her mouth. But to Mama, she was a perfect rose from God with not one single thorn.

"You're my princess." Mama said to Violet. "One day your prince will find you and give you a house full of love. Your sons will be olive shoots around your table; your daughters statues adorning a temple."

"But what about Rosie, Mama? What will happen to her?"

"She's my little queen who will sit by my side all the days of her life, blameless and pure, a child of God."

Violet looked down at her apron, spattered with grease from the chicken. It was dark out now; snow was building up in the corners of the windowpanes. She looked at her reflection in the window and smoothed her hair back into her chignon. She'd better attend to Simone. What an odd twist of fate that here she was in a big fancy house with another girl who, if you didn't see the color of her skin, looked more like her twin than Rosie did. She and Simone stood eye to eye. Both were slender around the waist and hips—Violet because she worked so hard, Simone because she hardly ate. Simone's shoes fit her perfectly. Even her kid gloves—the ones she kept in the back of her top drawer—slipped on Violet's fingers like they'd been made for her. But they hadn't been. Everything was for Simone.

Violet and Simone came from towns that were no more than ten miles apart, but in different states, different worlds. Missouri and Kentucky shared a boundary on opposite sides of the Mississippi. They didn't share land, only mingled river bottom to river bottom, both taking their form from the same alluvial plain.

On Violet's Missouri side, the once swampy wilderness was now called the boot heel. It was the only home she knew until Mrs. Blankwell reached her through an advertisement in the St. Louis Dispatch that read: *excellent opportunity for young, well-mannered woman. Light housework, occasional kitchen duty, bucolic farmhouse setting on the Huron River.* Violet's mother had to look up the meaning of *bucolic* in the Complete Webster's Dictionary that rested open on its own stand in her employer Dr. Applebaum's study. *Bucolic: of or pertaining to shepherds; pastoral; rustic; rural.* That sounded nice. And so did Huron River. Violet's mother had seen the ad, right under her thumb, as she was husking corn one afternoon for the Applebaum's supper, corn she had picked herself from her own garden that morning. She had known right then and there that this ad was God's doing, that it was time to rip the husks off her oldest child and send Violet away, so shiny, bright, untouched, and sweet, into someone else's kitchen.

Kentucky, on the other hand, Simone's fatherland, was known for thoroughbreds and tobacco, for coal and bourbon and dark winding caves.

Violet rinsed the dirty peels from the potatoes and covered them with cold water. It was too early to put them on to boil. On a regular night six-thirty was cocktail hour in the library or living room, depending on the number. Dinner began at seven o'clock sharp. Of course Randolph ate in the kitchen with the help. He got to sit at the table while she and Ambra popped up and down like two fish on one bobber whenever Mrs. Blankwell shook her silver bell. Violet's job was to go find out what was wrong. She would swallow or spit out whatever was in her mouth, rush through the pantry smoothing the sides of her hair as she passed the glass-doored cupboards, push slowly through the swinging door, and stand meekly behind and to the left of the Mrs. B to receive her orders. Then with just a "Yes Ma'am" she reported back to Ambra and the two of them would hustle to make things right.

Randolph made up a kitchen game. When the bell tinkled they'd each get a guess: too hot, too cold, too much, too little. Overdone, underdone. Plain old done. Plain old inedible. But that didn't happen much; Ambra was a magician in the kitchen. There had only been one instance when the whole roast was deemed unfit for human consumption and Ambra had to fry up a pound of bacon and scramble a dozen eggs. To be fair, one time the bell brought good tidings, too. Mrs. Blankwell summoned Violet in to tell Ambra that the potato pancakes were even better than the ones her German grandmother used to make. Violet noticed tears in Mrs. Blankwell's eyes—and that the sherry bottle had been emptied that evening.

It was strange now to have Simone be the only one home. Would she want to sit in her usual place in the dining room or would she move to the head of the table, looking at her own reflection in the wide black windows? Would she ring Mrs. Blankwell's bell?

The buzzer sounded again. This time there were two long blasts. Violet curtsied at the kitchen clock and hurried out to the study.

Chapter 8

RANDOLPH HAD BEEN LISTENING TO MUSIC since before he was born. His mother was the organist for the Transcendental Unitarian Church of New Orleans, the oldest Unitarian congregation in Louisiana. She had been employed there for a year and a half before his father, a former but now liberated Presbyterian, had signed on as minister in 1922. He had fallen in love with her Vivaldi concertos and her silver thighs; she had fallen in love with his melodious baritone and his cleft chin. They were both nearing thirty and uncomfortable with insinuations of spinster- and bachelor-hood. So when passion roused her tangled curls one breezy night in May, they relinquished themselves to their own human form of a Trinity. Randolph was born nine months later.

His mother was an urn who poured herself into music. The organ was her fountain and she filled herself from it every day. The church organ was conveniently placed below the eastern-facing Tiffany window in the sanctuary. The stained glass red poppies and the mid-morning light lit her amber hair like Moses' burning bush. She swayed and swooned and shook loose tendrils, hunching her shoulders, arching her back, letting her whole being merge with the thunderous sound. Sunday attendance had gone way up ever since she was hired.

Perhaps because she practiced with such intensity for at least three hours every morning, she spent the rest of the day in her room with the shutters pulled while the hot Louisiana air churned above her in the ceiling fan.

Randolph and his parents lived next door to the church in the manse, a squat and mildewed stucco building with the smell of swamp in every room. It had an enclosed courtyard full of crumbling statues and overgrown bougainvillea that attracted stray cats like a wounded bird. The early morning mewing and late night mating made his mother bang on her bedroom wall. "Deliver me!" he would hear her cry. His room was next to hers; his Father's was across the hall. It was too hot to sleep with someone else, his parents told him. Besides, they were both insomniacs. The staccato of his father's typewriter was the restless rhythm of Randolph's dreams. And he often watched his mother pacing the courtyard in the moonlight, her long white gown draping her like one of the faux Greek statues that had been left there by previous occupants. They were a household of prowlers.

His mother called him her little Apollo, the god of music. As soon as he was big enough, she sat him by her side on the organ bench and entertained him with dancing fingers and swinging legs that crossed and uncrossed under her as she became her own partner in the torrent of music.

She made him sit by her side in her bed, also.

"Come to me, my little Apollo," she said. "My darling boy." She smelled of lily of the valley and cigarettes and gin. Her knee angled out from her dressing gown, pale like an uncooked sausage. "Here, next to me." She patted the sheet and pulled him close.

She took his hands in hers. "You have fingers from heaven," she said. "Long and straight. You have my hands. Hands made for music. Fingers of passion." She circled his fingers, one at a time, with her fingertips, and lightly, gently stroked them from the base to the tip and back again. He wanted to pull away. Her body was damp against his and the sheets felt rumpled and sticky under his tee shirt and shorts. He still had his sneakers on and worried about getting dirt in the bed.

"Music is the language of love, my little man. It ties one soul to another with a silver cord. Even the stars sing."

He had two mosquito bites on his ankle. He wanted to scratch them.

"Music rises out of your heart…" She let go of his fingers and placed her hand on his chest. He reached for his ankle. One of the bites had a scab.

"…out of your soul…" She slid her hand down to his belly.

"…out of your very being." Her hand cupped him. He stopped his scratching. He turned to stone.

"I'm going to tell you a secret," she whispered. "Something you will understand when you get older." She moved her lips to his ear, her hand heavy on him. The blades of the ceiling fan cut the air into pieces above him. "This is the secret of music. This is the power of life."

He sprang off the bed and ran out the door.

A wooden lattice pergola had been erected over a bench in one corner of the courtyard to make a shady spot, back before the cypress trees wrapped the whole house in their shroud. Ivy grew up the latticework creating a perfect blind: Randolph could look out in any direction without being seen. This was his sanctuary. This was his church. He had an old tackle box hidden under the stone bench where he kept his carefully acquired treasures. For although his parents were Unitarians, he waxed sacramental, verging on voodoo.

In his box was a cut glass perfume bottle he pilfered from his mother's vanity. But the Lily of the Valley was nearly eradicated by a sour, yellowish liquid he had filled it with himself. Strands of her hair wound tight around a screw he had removed from the underside of his father's typewriter. From the powder room wastebasket at church he scavenged a rubbery clamp-like thing that women used to hold up their stockings. He had retrieved his father's old shaving brush and cut off the boar bristles with a razor blade—he had swiped a whole box of those from the janitor's closet at church—and stuck the bristles into the candle stubs left over from the winter solstice service. Of course he had matches, shiny pennies, shards of colored glass, and bits of fabric snipped from the edges of parishioners' shawls, his father's holy vestments, and his mother's nightgowns.

What was he doing with these slightly illicit yet seemingly harmless tokens of the adult world? He didn't know. He was simply following an unnamed impulse that drove him from dark corner to dark corner, into rooms that were unofficially off limits, gathering odd remnants like ingredients for a powerful potion or spell.

One of the local stray cats would not leave him alone. Randolph couldn't tell if it was male or female, but its ginger fur was the same color as his mother's hair. The same color as his. He hated that cat. It always knew when he was in his secret place and would come running, silently, on padded feet and rub its snaky body against his shin. The more he shoved it away, even kicked at it, the more tenacious the cat became. He thought of tying it in a bag with stones and dropping it in the Mississippi. But it was a long walk to the river and someone might see him. He obsessed over the cat until one hot afternoon, after he'd taken his mother a lunch tray of canned tuna on saltines and a pitcher of iced tea, he knew what to do.

It was a horrible thing, something most people would not want to think about. But Randolph thought it and then he did it. He set the empty tuna fish can inside the pergola and waited. When the cat came, as he knew it would, he grabbed it and held it between his knees. Then he unwrapped the thin veneer of human decency that hid the double-edged depravity of his soul, a blade of violence honed sharp by the twin demons of religious and sexual abuse. When he let the cat go, it stood at his feet, back arched, trying to howl. No sound came from its mouth. It disappeared forever under the back gate.

The courtyard was strangely silent for weeks after that, as if all the felines in the neighborhood knew that something unthinkable, an utter sacrilege had been committed. It had. Lucky for Randolph he wasn't living in ancient Egypt where harming a cat was a capital offence.

Dividing a house into separate dwellings does not require
nearly the skill of building a house in the first place.
Creativity takes far more planning than does deconstruction.

Chapter 9

THE SNOW WAS A WHITE WHIRLING MASS outside the study window. Big wet flakes stuck to the mullions. Simone could just barely see a small glow from the lamp-post on the walk outside the front door. It was going to be a big storm. A giant storm. A wrap-yourself-in-an-afghan and drink hot chocolate kind of storm. Where was Violet? Simone tugged on the cord again. Twice, for good measure. Instead of tea she would have a pot of cocoa with plenty of marshmallows. And a plate of those shortbread cookies she liked so well.

She arranged herself on the window seat, tucking her feet under her skirt, and looked at the still life she'd started this afternoon at her class at the Women's City Club. It needed more shadow under the table and behind the bottles. She always marveled at how a little bit of darkness made other things jump into the light. Almost like magic. Maybe that was the spice of life Lincoln was always talking about.

She wondered if it was snowing in Illinois, too. Lincoln should be calling soon. He promised to call her every night. Would he still be out on the road? His sports car was so small and light, even with the sandbags he carried in the trunk. But he was an impeccable driver. At least that's what he said. And he knew all about his car—even the extra gas tank. She rested her head against the cold glass. It was completely dark out now. The shade on the table lamp was tilted a bit and the twin bulbs glowed as tiny reflections in the window. They looked like headlights in the distance, like the headlights of the tow truck that had been driving out to help them that night last fall when Lincoln ran out of gas.

They had been to dinner with the "Spooks"—that was the name of the Ann Arbor crowd she'd been adopted into when she married Lincoln. No one would tell her where the name came from. Not even Lincoln. "After you've been here a year—then you'll know." They had laughed at her. They were just a bunch of grown children, big fish in a little pond.

The Spooks and their spouses were a close and rowdy crowd. They got together nearly every weekend. In the fall they had tailgate parties with plenty of booze to keep them warm during the long football games at the big stadium. Once the river froze, they had skating parties with a bonfire on shore and beer packed in the snow banks. It was lots of fun, or at least she told herself it should be. Everyone was laughing, hugging, sometimes kissing. Lots of whoops and hollers went on, crack the whip and snow tag. Even staid old Lincoln joined it, sort of. He wouldn't skate, of course not. Too much like dancing which he pooh-poohed. Or maybe, she suspected, he didn't want to be outshone and he certainly wouldn't want to take the chance of falling down and looking like a fool. Instead he stood by the fire with the handful of other stiffs who were too sophisticated for frolicking. They'd huddle together discussing politics or the stock market or something boring while the rest of the gang dashed and wobbled across the ice. Some of the Spooks were surprisingly deft. Simone loved to skate, loved to dance, loved anything dreamy where she could close her eyes and forget about other people, forget about the ideas she was supposed to have opinions about. When she was moving around a room or a rink or even the river —especially with other moving bodies—she could almost make herself believe she belonged.

The night of the tow truck they had been at the Chelsea Inn with six or eight others from their group. Dinner had gone on and on. An hour of cocktails, then appetizers, wine with dinner, dessert, spiked coffee, after-dinner drinks. Then cigars and more than one bottle of port. Lincoln and the others had reminisced over stories from their common childhood: stealing old man Barton's Cadillac on Halloween, sneaking a sack full of bats into the State Theater and them letting them go in front of the projection booth, wrapping rubber bands around the snouts of their dogs, or using clothes pins to tie dog tails together until they rolled and scratched and whined. Near the end of dinner Lincoln stood up and clanged his glass to inform everyone that port got its name because it was from Portugal. He liked knowing things he thought other people didn't know. But he hadn't known about the extra gas tank in his BMW Roadster until they ran out of gas on their way home.

Lincoln never caravanned home with the rest of the Spooks. For one thing, they drove too close to the speed limit. For another, they didn't hold their liquor like he did. He was smooth and in control no matter how much he drank. He would instruct Simone to dawdle in the powder room so they could be the last ones to leave—and the first ones to get home. He liked to take the back roads, especially at night, so he could check out his acceleration and practice banking on sharp country curves. But the night of the dinner party the car came to a standstill all on its own, out in the middle of nowhere, on a road that ran between a cornfield and a pumpkin patch.

"Damn," was the first word out of his mouth.

"Ooh Linc, look at the moon," Simone said. An evening of alcohol left her feeling very relaxed and in the mood. She wanted to rest her head on his shoulder. But Lincoln shrugged her off and tried the key in the ignition again. The engine turned over but it wouldn't start.

"I bet the pathetic tank is empty." He opened his door and jumped out. "Have you been driving my car without permission?" he shouted as he lifted the hood.

"No Linc." She rolled down her window and leaned out. "But it's kind of romantic out here. Listen, I hear a hoot owl."

"Hand me the flashlight from under the seat. I'm going to walk back to that farm we just passed and use their phone."

She handed it to him, then slid down in her seat and propped her head against the doorframe.

Ten minutes later he was back.

"Tow truck's on its way," he said looking under the hood again.

"Linc, come back inside with me."

He fiddled around with the flashlight when all of a sudden he slapped the side of the car and let out a whoop. "Slide over and try the ignition," he said. "I think this beautiful baby has a reserve tank."

The car started right up. He hopped in, revved the engine, and they sped off.

"What about the tow truck?" she asked. "Didn't you say it was on its way?"

"Those Germans got some things right." He moved quickly through the gears. "Listen to that pussy purr."

"Lincoln." She was wide-awake now. The fields rushed past her window. "Not so fast. And what about the tow truck? It's after midnight. You must have gotten someone out of bed."

"Just the farmer's wife and that dolt from AAA. Hey look, here he comes now."

From the top of a slight rise in the distance they could see two headlights bumping along the dirt road. Lincoln down shifted and turned onto a tractor path, putting out his headlights as he pulled to a stop.

"But...." Before she could protest, he was all over her, laughing his silent laugh and letting her know she belonged to him.

A short knock on the study door and the flash of a blue uniform reminded Simone she was hungry and tired of waiting.

"You rang Miss Simone?" Violet blushed when she saw the new watercolor taped on the window seat behind Simone's head. Was that girl going to put those things all over the house? Back home they only had one picture in the house: a dark-skinned Jesus standing outside a lighted house, knocking on the door. Mama treated it like a shrine.

"I certainly did. And more than once." Simone stood and paused, hoping to see the girl squirm. "I'd like some hot chocolate. Drostes. And a bowl of marshmallows. And a plate of those shortbread cookies Mrs. Blankwell's sister sent from England."

"Yes Ma'am," Violet bobbed. "Will that be all?"

"Heavens, you don't need to do that."

"Do what Ma'am?"

"Genuflect, or whatever that is you're doing. We're not in church and I'm not the queen."

"Yes Ma'am." Violet turned her head away. Not the queen, just the princess.

"And what about dinner?" Simone asked. Why did this girl make her feel so uncomfortable? All the other coloreds in her life had made her feel special. And safe. More special and much safer than even her family and friends. Except for Toby. Toby MacIntire. He had made her feel more than special. Their bedroom windows faced each other's across Swan Street back home. They were best friends from the day he moved into the neighborhood when he was six and she was four. For her fifth birthday he gave her a toy pistol with a pearl handle. He let her play outfield with his baseball buddies even though she couldn't throw the ball all the way to home plate. On summer evenings they'd sit together on his front porch drinking homemade root beer. Toby would rub the cold bottle against his forehead while she pressed hers between her bare legs. That was until the summer Toby's father got put in jail for making bathtub gin. Then they drank Dr. Pepper at her house and watched fireflies darting through the summer sweet and bridal bouquet. Her side porch was more private anyway. When he was fourteen Toby learned to play the guitar and he wrote songs for her, beautiful songs with words that hinted at secrets and melodies that wrapped around her like a gentle breeze. But now Toby was only a shadow, a melancholy dream that woke her too many mornings with a knot in her throat.

"Dinner at seven, Ma'am?" Violet asked, startling her.

"Of course," Simone said.

"In the dining room?" Simone bristled at these questions. Violet had such an annoying way of honing in on Simone's insecurities. Her words sounded polite, but made Simone unsure of herself. Even the neat piles of folded clothes left on the window seat in her room felt like a slap in the face. And the way she lined up the cigarettes and lighter next to the crystal ashtray on the side table made them seem like objects on an altar of sin. Violet was a strange, silent girl and not to be trusted. Simone wouldn't be at all surprised if there was hanky-panky going on between Violet and Randolph. She knew they whispered about her when they thought they were alone. She caught them exchanging glances—even touches—just yesterday. They probably had some elaborate game they played, making fun of her and Lincoln. Well, they were just jealous. She would keep herself above all that. She was

Mrs. Blankwell, Jr. Someday this would be her house. And for the next three days she was in charge.

"Of course," she said again. "In the dining room. At seven. As usual."

Violet turned to go.

"And Violet." She said the girl's name so fast it almost sounded like violent. "I'll have my cocoa in the living room. At the piano. I'm going to play."

Chapter 10

RANDOLPH BUTTONED HIS SHIRT and fastened his watch. He hooked his wire-rimmed glasses behind his ears and looked at his wrist. Almost six. He would go over to the house early, before dinner, so he could be alone with Violet. Ambra was in Detroit, the Blankwells were all away except for Simone, and she didn't count. He could blow her over with one little puff. He arched his back and grinned. I'll huff and I'll puff and I'll blow your house in.

He spun the top of the Baldwin's stool as he passed it on the way to the door. He would much prefer a bench, like the shiny black one at the Steinway in the Blankwell's living room. Then he could move with the music, slide up and down the scale, use his body like his mother used hers at the organ. Yes! he thought. That's just what he'd do. Since no one one was home, he'd play in the big house tonight. Violet wouldn't stop him and Simone couldn't stop him. These next few days were going to be fun.

He grabbed his pipe and tobacco tin—another trespass Mrs. B. would never discover—and stuck them in the pocket of his shirt. He pulled his sweater over his head and checked his mustache in the mirror before putting on his coat. Usually he'd just run down the stairs, past the garage, under the breezeway, and over to the mudroom door without a coat, but the snow had not let up. He had to push hard against the door to get it open. More than a foot of snow was already banked against it. Shoveling was going to be pure drudgery, but he'd wait until the storm was over. No one was going anywhere tonight. He grinned again as he reached back inside to grab his red knit hat and gloves, then half-slid down the stairs into the stormy night.

Even though the garage was attached to the house by the breezeway, the upstairs rooms where Randolph lived had no direct entry into the main building. Instead they were reached from a steep set of stairs on the east end of the garage. Those upper rooms used to be a rumpus room for Lincoln—ping pong table, dart board, foosball, a trunk with his Boy Scout gear on top and girly magazines underneath—but when he went away to school his mother turned it into an apartment for the gardener. She'd hung gingham curtains decorated with rick-rack from the dormer windows, brought over an old braided rug, and installed plenty of hooks along the wall for clothes. What had been a closet in the small sleeping room she'd made into a proper W.C., then put a sink in the main room. Not an arrangement she would have approved of for herself, but she wouldn't be the one living there.

Randolph trudged through snow up to his knees. The wind battered him, drove snow under his collar and down into his boots. The sound of the storm was deafening, a cacophony of kettledrums and howling strings. He could barely make out the shape of the house and the faint glow from the kitchen windows. Wind roared around the corner of the porch; sheets of snow blew down from the roof as if heaven was shaking out its laundry. He clambered up the steps and pulled hard to get the storm door open. This was a true Shakespearean Ides of March.

Once inside he leaned against the mudroom door to catch his breath and wipe the steam from his lenses. If the snow didn't stop soon, he'd be stuck in the house. He grinned a third time. He was full of good ideas tonight. He hung up his things, took off his boots, and tiptoed into the kitchen. It was warm and bright and smelled of fried chicken and baking biscuits. A bowl of last summer's strawberries was defrosting on the table. Short cake, he thought. Maybe whipped cream. He'd stumbled on a gold mine of good food when he took on this job. The kitchen was empty but a can of cocoa and a box of cookies lay open on the counter. Violet must be waiting on her highness. He sat down at the table and put his stocking feet on a chair. The pantry door swung open.

"Randolph."

He loved to hear Violet say his name. Her voice was a deep clarinet—no, a high oboe. She resonated with a double reed. Two impulses came from her lips and he aimed to find both of them.

"A mighty tempest blows outside," he said. "The gods are angry tonight. Have you been neglecting your prayers?"

"Take your feet off that chair," she said as she gave the

strawberries a stir, popping one in her mouth. "And you'd better be sure there's plenty of dry wood in the firebox."

"I filled it yesterday, remember?" He loved to make her blush, adding a touch of red to her maple syrup skin. "Don't fret, Violet. I'll keep you warm."

The awkward sounds of a butchered "Maple Leaf Rag" rang out from the living room. They looked at each other. "I hope she doesn't get all worked up and spill hot choc-olate on the piano," Violet said. "That's just what I don't need."

"Worry, not" Randolph said. "When she's playing—or trying to play—Scott Joplin it's a sign she's happy. When she starts in on Debussy, that's when you have to watch out."

"What makes you think you know everything?" she asked, trying not to show that he impressed her.

"I've been trapped here all winter just like you."

She lifted the lid on the pan of chicken. Fat spattered and hissed as she turned the pieces over. "I'm cooking extra, in case this storm keeps going and we can't get to the grocery. Shouldn't you be shoveling? There's plenty of time to clear the walks before dinner."

"I'll shovel that food into my belly first. There's no sense working up a sweat before the snow stops. Besides, she isn't expecting company, is she?"

"I doubt it," Violet said as she took a pan of biscuits from the oven. He leaned back in his chair and swiped one.

"Stop, you thief." She slapped at his hand but he'd already popped the hot biscuit into his mouth. Then, in one motion, he grabbed her wrist and tried to pulled her into his lap. The sudden movement made her drop the pan, and as she lunged for the biscuits scattered on the floor, he lost his balance and tumbled backwards, making Violet land on top of him. They broke into laughter. The piano stopped.

"Hush," Violet said, untangling herself. "Next thing you know she'll be in here wondering what's going on."

"And catch us in the act," he said. He took hold of her shoulders as she tried to get up. For a moment she looked him straight in the eye and he saw his own reflection against the bittersweet chocolate of her iris and the bottomless black of her pupil. "You know you want me," he said.

"Like a snake bite," she answered, but too late. He pressed his rough face into hers and tasted her lips. Strawberries.

"Get off and get out!" she cried, stumbling away from him.

He righted himself and picked up another biscuit from the floor. "Just call me when you're ready," he said and left through the narrow passage that led from the kitchen, past the telephone room, and into the hall. From there he could see the piano and the back of anyone sitting on its bench.

Chapter 11

THE LIVING ROOM WAS MAGNIFICENT, Mrs. Blankwell's triumph de vivre. It ran the entire width of the house, from north to south, with a fireplace at each end. In the middle of this expanse, across from the front entryway, stood the grand circular staircase. Hung would be a better verb than stood, for this elaborate feat of carpentry seemed suspended from above, an opulent twist on Jacob's ladder—without the angels.

In the northwest corner of the house sat the study. That was Simone's favorite room, though she could hardly be thought of as studious. She had muddled her way through Louisville Country Day and had only completed one year at Marymount Finishing School. Her education was far from finished. In the southwest corner of the house was the library, home of the spinning globe that had been suspended forever in Simone's recent watercolor. Adjoining the library was the sunroom and beyond that, outdoors, in the sheltered crook between the south wall of the house and the sunroom was the scholar's garden, Mrs. Blankwell's pride and joy.

Study, library, scholar's garden. One would think the old farmhouse was full of knowledge. But it was a veneer of culture and a certain sophistication of class—built like a pyramid on the luck and hard labor of Mrs. Blankwell, Sr.'s father—that defined the scheme of the house. One runaway farm boy who found himself in the right place at the right time had set up a legacy that—with prudence—could last for generations.

Unlike Simone, Mrs. Blankwell excelled at her New England boarding school and finished four years at one of the Seven Sisters. To top off her education in a manner quite in vogue in certain circles at the time, Harriet's parents sent her and her sister, chaperoned by a maiden aunt, by train to San Francisco, and then by steamer to the Orient for a first-hand look at the other side the world. The girls spent several weeks in China and Harriet developed a curiosity for the ancient city of Suzhou with its classical 15th century gardens of spectacular architecture and dramatic plantings. Once settled in her own home she spared no cost to recreate a miniature world of land and water on the backside of the 19th century farmhouse. The lotus pond and the mosaic pathway were not the only signs of the Orient at Harriet's house: The dining room was wallpapered with the bamboo-patterned squares of paper that had once lined boxes of imported tea. A collection of miniature Yixing teapots in whimsical shapes sat in a lighted glass case. Next to the sofa in the north end of the living room was a set of black lacquered nesting tables with feet shaped like the heads of dragons. And across from the piano, which was in an alcove behind the stairs, was a large Korean chest, stout and strong like a warrior, with shiny brass hinges and gold-leaf doors.

Simone lifted the heavy top of the piano and rested it on the lid prop. She lit the candelabra, all five candles, to keep her company and to shoo away the distracting noises coming from the kitchen. She hated being left alone. Lincoln was so insensitive. Didn't he know how hard it was for her to be stranded in his family's house while he was galavanting across the country? And until last month before his parents went on their trans-Atlantic cruise, she'd had to spend every day listening to their bickering and small talk. Then she'd had to sit through cocktails and tedious dinners with his parents and their friends when all she wanted was to be alone with Linc, to have him read her stories from *The Saturday Evening Post*, while she snuggled with him in bed. Now everyone was gone and she was mistress-by-default.

She started to play a ragtime tune, but couldn't get the rhythm quite right. Voices came from the kitchen. She imagined Randolph and Violet laughing at her, trying to make her feel like a fool. She did feel foolish at the piano, especially since Randolph moved in. She was an amateur but he was a pro. Sometimes she sneaked out to the garage and stood beneath his windows listening to the emotions he created with his fingers.

Suddenly there was a loud crash in the kitchen followed by peals of laughter. She pulled her hands away from the keys and put them in her lap. Those two were doing their best to make her feel left out and remind her she was all alone. Why didn't Lincoln call?

She gazed at the candles and thought back to a bright afternoon in the fall when her marriage was still new, when she had loved having this big house all to herself. She adored the way the living room went from one end of the house to the other, how it looked out over the lawn, down the elm-lined drive, across the road, and over the river. The town of Ann Arbor sat on the other side like a European fortress. Even though the farmhouse was in the country, she could sometimes hear the University's bell tower chiming the hours, and imagined it to be a sister song from another Rapuntzel. She would sit at the piano and match the notes of the carillon—B flat two octaves below middle C. The boom, boom, boom resonated in the hollow place between her ribs, the cage that held her heart.

She gave up on Scott Joplin and began a minor chord progression down the scale. It was part of an old duet her mother had taught her. The dark dissonance fit her mood and reminded her of someone lost in a cave. That's how she felt, like she had climbed down from the bright years of girlhood through the narrow door of marriage and into a cold, damp place. She just hoped that if she kept walking, kept whistling in the dark, she'd catch a spot of light and find the way out.

She played the bottom part of the duet over a few more times, then started in on the top. How did it go? F, F, E, D#, C#? She fumbled and tried again. From the corner of her eye she saw a match blaze and smelled a pipe. Randolph. He was in the room. She stopped playing and sat still, listening as he sucked on the pipe to get it going. She knew the procedure only too well from her father. But smoking a pipe was strictly taboo in the Blankwell house. Her mother-in-law called it a filthy *southern* habit, so Randolph better look out.

"I know that piece," he said. "'The Dance of the Druids' according to my mother but I doubt that's its proper name. Shall we have a go together?"

She felt his warm exhalation and realized Randolph was standing behind her. He moved close to her left side; she slid up the bench to let him sit down.

"Alright," she said. "But I'm not sure about the melody."

His pipe smoke combined with the cloyingly sweet hot chocolate was making her feel dizzy.

He reached his arm behind her and played the top part. F, F, E, D#, D. That was it. His body was warm. Then he tweaked C# and C together, just like her mother used to. It gave her the chills, two notes so close together, yet dissonant. Even though there was no harmony, it still sounded good. It had a power all its own.

"Thanks," she said. "Now I remember." She leaned away and he withdrew his arm.

"I'll begin," he said, holding his pipe with his teeth. To heck with his sore thumb. This was an opportunity he wouldn't miss. "You join when you want." He talked out of the side of his mouth just like her father and she felt a tremor of homesickness.

Randolph was a genius at the piano, even with such a simple song. He coaxed the keys to sing together like a choir. His tempo was never stiff, but full of subtle halts and starts that caught her off guard. He must be a sensitive man underneath his brusque manner. She watched as his head danced, moving back and forth, up and down. No, no. Yes, yes. As he came to the end of the phrasing, he nodded to her.

She started the melody with one hand and got all the way through without a mistake.

"Good," he said. "Now move up an octave and try both hands."

She had to concentrate at first, but soon memory took over. She had played this piece for hours when she was a girl. It was a dreamy, gothic, mesmerizing piece that made her feel like Eustacia Vye in *Return of the Native*. It brought to mind moors and heaths and ancient runes. Randolph slowed it down, then sped it up. He intensified the volume with his foot on the pedal. His right leg only flexed up and down a little, but enough for her to feel the current of music passing between them. She followed every move, every mood, like partners in a dance. She let her right hand drift up the register and played in a high, haunting voice.

"I like that," he said. "It does have an aura of Druids, doesn't it?" He reached over and played in between her hands.

"Druids?" What exactly were they, she wondered.

"You know, mistletoe and sacred oak trees—like the big one in the backyard." His pipe rattled against his teeth. "Druids worshipped at Stonehenge on winter and summer solstice. Spring and fall equinox, too. Just about this time of year."

He was sitting too close. The muscles in his forearms stood taut like strings across a sounding board. Their moving hands reflected in the shiny surface of the piano like blurry ghosts. She felt claustrophobic. His pipe smoke was thick and sweet. She wanted to stop this eerie song, to switch to "Chop Sticks" or "Heart and Soul"—no, not "Heart and Soul"—yet the minor chords kept pulling her in.

"The Druids believed the soul was immortal," he said, "and entered a new body after death." His thigh was next to hers. She felt it tighten as he pressed his foot against the pedal, sustaining notes, then mixing them all up together. "That's what my mother believed. How about you? Haven't you ever felt like you've lived other lives before this one?"

"Sometimes," she said. She knew what he was talking about. So many times, lying in her bed at night, or out on the lawn watching clouds drift by, or daydreaming by the window—and especially when she was painting—she felt as if she were melding into someone else or something else. Or maybe that someone else was slipping into her. She wasn't good at expressing ideas. They were only feelings to her, not words. And Lincoln—the thought of him made her miss a note—would laugh if she ever brought up something so ethereal, so non-scientific.

"Druids killed animals," he said "and dissected their remains to predict the future. They studied the flights of birds, too." She thought of her watercolors up in her room: the oak tree and the cardinal in flight. "Some people claim they even sacrificed humans."

With a jerk she pulled her hands into her lap and Randolph stopped playing. She felt her heart pounding and inched away from him. "I need to get ready for dinner."

"Right," he said. "It's going to be delicious. Bright red strawberries for dessert. I had a taste."

"Oh you did? Was that the racket I heard?" She stood

and cupped her hand behind one candle at a time as she blew them out.

"No, that was the biscuits. Violet gave me a sample of her treats."

The room was dark now except for the light coming down the hall from the kitchen. And the glow of his pipe. They both moved away from the bench at the same time and collided. Her arm hit his hand and knocked his pipe to the floor.

"Sorry," she said.

He went down on his knees.

"Watch the carpet," she said. The piano stood on an antique Oriental rug.

"I've got it," he said and caught her ankle in the circle of his fingers.

"That's me," she shrieked.

"Ah, so it is." He slipped his fingers inside her sock.

"Let go you brute," she said and kicked at him.

He laughed. "Not so cold on the inside, are you?"

She sprang away and ran up the stairs to her room.

*When the house mover is called, the first thing he does
is inspect the underside of the house to determine how it
is put together. He examines the joists running from one
foundation wall to the other, or, on older homes, looks to
see how hand-hewed timbers sit on top of foundation stones.*

Chapter 12

RANDOLPH STOOD STILL IN THE LIVING ROOM, the stummel of his pipe was growing cold in his palm. The light from the hall chandelier clothed him in striped shadows as it passed through the banister of the staircase. Simone had flipped the switch on her flight upstairs. He could hear Violet in the kitchen where pans and cupboard doors were making more noise than usual. But dinner smelled good. He was looking forward to more strawberries.

He walked to the south end of the big room, stepping around side tables and chintz-covered chairs, careful not to trip over Mrs. B's scattered collection of hooked rugs. He noticed she didn't go in for much that was new, but liked to surround herself with the patina of age. He had never been in this room alone, at least not to enjoy it, only as a servant filling the beaten brass bucket with logs for the fire or standing on the stepladder to change a light bulb.

But what was to stop him tonight from being master of the house? He'd always wanted to sit in one of the overstuffed chairs by the fire with his feet on an ottoman. To smoke his pipe and sip a glass of sherry—or better yet a shot of Scotch. He'd like to take his place at the head of the long cherry table in the dining room and gaze through candlelight at a beautiful woman or two, feel the heft of sterling silver in his hands, slice through rare lamb and asparagus with hollandaise sauce. Why not do it now? Why not have their own Twelfth Night, exchange places with the master? This chance might never come again.

He settled for a finger of bourbon from the cut-crystal decanter and settled himself into old Mr. B's favorite chair. Comfy, indeed, he thought as he emptied his rather expensive briar pipe—a gift to himself for surviving the war—and began his ritual over again: pinching and packing the bowl with fresh tobacco from the pouch in his breast pocket, charring and tamping for a nice, even surface, then finally lighting up for some long, deep draws. This was the life, he thought, a life that could be his one day if his strategy unfolded as planned.

He reached over and lit a candle on the table next to him and gazed at the flame. It was odd, really, how that crooked wick, bent and black, a mere twisting of cheap fibers buried at the core of some paraffin, could produce such radiance, such glory. It hardly did anything at all, was just an inert piece of string except for the orange glow at its tip where little by little it gave itself up and steadily disappeared. The wick was just a conduit, a sacrificial element, yet it was somehow noble, bridging the gap between fire and wax.

He looked harder at the flame in front of him. It swayed and danced, oblivious in this well-built room to the fierce gusts of wind outside. It shrunk down a bit into itself, then stretched tall and thin, reaching for the ceiling. If he tilted his head and relaxed his eyes, focusing not on the flame but on the middle ground in front of it, he could see what before had been invisible—a golden globe, an aura, a halo around the flame. Vibrating waves of smoky heat radiated out from the center of combustion. Or was it a trick of his eye, a conjunction of unfocused lens and peripheral retina making him see in 3D?

An old *Michigan Daily*, folded open to the movie page, lay on the shelf under the table next to him. Frank Capra's *It's a Wonderful Life* was opening that weekend at the State Theater downtown. But there was also a rerun of Cecil B. De Mille's *The Ten Commandments*. He'd like to see it again, even if it was a silent film. Maybe he could take Violet tomorrow if the storm let up. Maybe even Simone would deign go with them. He loved the story of Moses, his face turning brilliant—like a candle himself—after he talked to God on Mt. Sinai. He loved how Moses threw down the first tablets in disgust when he saw the Israelites having an orgy in front of the golden calf. When Randolph was a boy he thumbed through his father's books in the church library and read about people from the Old Testament, like the Canaanites. They were quite a society, having sex with cows and sacrificing their sons and daughters. Their priests and priestesses were temple prostitutes, and the only way to make the gods happy and make sure your crops were good was to make a lot of trips to the temple. The Bible was full of great stories: blood and gore, incest and rape.

The Transcendental Unitarian Church of New Orleans where he grew up was a melting pot for people with spiritual inclinations, but an aversion to orthodox theology. No "Thou shalt nots" or "Thus says the Lords." The French influence was strong and laissez-faire was their creed. In his father's church, along with the sentimentalists and existentialists who sat side by side enjoying his mother's Sunday morning organ concerts, the church also attracted its share of quacks who left their marks in the sanctuary: A kneeling pillow depicting an upside-down crucified St. Peter in vivid petit-point. Or the sterling silver candlestick on the base of a sphinx. Randolph's favorite was a miniature replica of the Tabernacle, complete with a gold-covered Ark of the Covenant behind a linen veil in the Holy of Holies.

The model of the Tabernacle was five feet wide and ten feet long. Its builder was the chief financial donor to the church, so his gift stood on a platform at one end of the social hall, facing east, protected under a Plexiglass cover suspended from a pulley on the ceiling. On the wall next to the Tabernacle hung an annotated diagram explaining each article of furniture and illustrating in bright detail the slaughtered animals complete with a generous sprinkling of blood.

As a boy Randolph's fascination was with animal sacrifices and priestly rituals. He would sneak over to the social hall on muggy afternoons and hoist the top off the Tabernacle. Then he would peer through the one door into the outer court, picturing himself entering into the Jewish rituals. Standing on a chair he could lean into the panorama over the brass altar with its four brass horns, one on each corner, where the animal bodies were tied crossways above the fire and grate. It was like a fancy barbecue, a pig roast on Mardi Gras. He saw smoke rising above the hot coals and he imagined the aroma of roasting flesh. He fingered the fancy material of the drapes hanging in the doorway and pricked his fingers on the sharp tips of the horns.

He saw himself dressed like the high priest in the diagram—covered in gold and blue and purple and red linen with a breastplate of twelve stones across his chest. He pretended to wash his bloody hands in the bronze bowl, then go into the Tabernacle proper, the tiny two-room house in the back of the courtyard. It was like the pergola back at the manse, and his tackle box, hidden under the stone bench, was his Ark of the Covenant.

A creak in the ceiling above shifted him back to the present. Simone must be wandering through the master bedroom. It was nearly seven. She would be coming down for dinner soon. He snuffed out the candle with two fingers and headed for the kitchen. No need to startle Simone with his new position in the household. He would break the news to her gently.

Chapter 13

SIMONE WAS RELIEVED TO GET BACK TO HER ROOM, to her private corner of the house with her own things: her chaise, her cigarettes, and her deep clawfoot tub. She wished she had time for a soak but it was nearly seven and she could tell Violet was making a fuss over dinner. It wouldn't be right to stay in her room a second night in a row, not with Randolph behaving so strangely. It was as if he had brought the storm right into the house with him.

She pulled off her bobby socks and tossed them in a corner, then plopped into the feather pillows on the chaise and buried her toes under the throw. Why hadn't Lincoln called? He must be back to his hotel by now. Or at a restaurant. She didn't even know where he was staying. Violet said he hadn't left a return number when she took his call last night. Where could he be? Who was he with? She needed a cigarette to calm her nerves. A swig of bourbon wouldn't hurt either. Maybe vodka would be smarter. She wouldn't want Violet—or Randolph—to smell her breath. There was a stack of books on the lower shelf of the side table. She reached down for the fattest one. *The Collected Poems of W. B. Yeats.* She chose it for her secret cache knowing Lincoln would never be tempted to lift the cover. Inside the book, with a razor blade, she had carefully slit out the center of each page. It had been hard work and taken nearly an afternoon, but it was well worth a bruised finger and thumb. She extracted the silver flask fitted snug inside and gave herself a little pick-me-up, as her mother-in-law would say.

What should she do tonight? It was such a bore to be alone. Maybe she'd light a fire, or—she corrected herself—have a fire lit. She'd been wanting to look through the new Van Gogh book Lincoln gave her for Christmas. She could pick out a painting or two and copy them tomorrow when the light was good. She took another swig, screwed on the cap, and tucked her secret back in its hiding place. She felt even drowsier. Was there time for a little nap? She pulled the blanket behind her shoulder and closed her eyes.

She thought of hot summer afternoons in Missouri when her mother made her lay down next to her on the high four-poster bed in the downstairs guest room. It was the only time Mother spent just with her. "First one asleep whistle," she always said as she slipped her black satin eye patch over her forehead and fell right to sleep.

Lying still Simone would wait. Eleven, twelve whistles escaped from the lump beside her. Twenty-four, twenty-five. Her mother sounded like a teakettle nearly out of water. Then Simone would slide carefully to the floor and creep out the French doors, scurrying barefoot to the old lot beyond the fence where their cook's two little boys played in the dirt.

"Shouldn yous be nappin, Miss Simone?" said one.

"You're not," she said.

"Bes gits yer switch now and saves trouble later," said the other. The boys knew as well as Simone that when her mother awoke and found her missing, she would force Simone to reenact her daily punishment: cutting her own switch—no thinner than her mother's thumb—and bending over the foot stool in the parlor to receive her lashes.

Wind pounding at the windows brought her back to the cold North. Ivy scratched against the panes. Simone got up to pull the drapes but stopped when she noticed that her watercolors were out of order. She was positive she'd tucked the one she painted of Violet behind the other two. She looked around the room: Violet had done a sloppy job straightening up today. The edge of her robe and nightgown were pinched in the closet door. What did that girl think she was doing? Had she been snooping around in her things? This was serious. That girl needed a talking to.

Simone undid the brass buttons on her cardigan and unzipped her wool skirt. At least she didn't have to dress for dinner tonight. Instead she'd dress down, make herself comfortable, make herself at home. In fact, she'd wear her mother-in-law's Japanese kimono, the one with the peacock on the back. Mrs. Blankwell never wore it, she just showed it off at cocktail parties, draping it over the sofa. It needed a warm body inside to bring the bird to life.

She sashayed down the hall in bare feet and slip, past the stairway, through the master bedroom, and into the dressing room where she switched on the light. It was a clever room with wallpaper on every wall and even the ceiling. The closet doors were flush with the walls and papered to match. She had to look carefully to see the small wooden knobs—also covered with paper—that were the only sign of a door. There were two closets on each of the four walls. She didn't know which were whose but soon found out that her father-in-law had more than enough suits to go around. And two dozen or more sweaters neatly folded on shelves covered with the same rose-pink paper. Her mother-in-law's sweaters—she favored thin cashmere with lace or beaded flowers appliquéd across the bodice and down one arm—were housed in clear plastic boxes with lids.

In a closet next to the fireplace she came across a bevy of garment bags and found the kimono hanging regally on a plushly padded hanger. Everything reeked of Shalimar. She left the hanger on a chair and wrapped the silky robe around her body, tying its dark red sash tight at her waist. She went into the adjoining bathroom and turned on the light. The shimmering silk made her skin look even paler than usual, like a porcelain doll, a Japanese geisha. The deep blues made her eyes shine azure. The red at her waist reflected her lips. She scooped her dark hair down over one eye—like a naughty Veronica Lake. Not bad. She'd have to dress up like this for Lincoln when he got home. He loved her in turquoise, he always said.

She rushed back to her room, the long arms of the gown flying out behind her like wings. She was Peter Pan. She wanted to fly. She wanted to find Never-Never Land.

She had always been a theatrical girl. She found it more fun playing other people than being herself. Beginning in fourth grade, when she sprouted a half head taller than the other girls, she won a role in the Louisville Country Day's annual "Spring Fever Productions." Miss Eloise Brown, headmistress at LCD, had been educated at Barnard and spent the next years of her life directing summer stock around New England and producing Broadway revivals in Fort Lauderdale in the winters. Even though the swimming pool at the school needed re-grouting and the stables needed a new roof, the drama department had both a proscenium stage and a theater-in-the-round, and the costume and prop rooms were the envy of the Louisville acting community. No expense was spared, no excuse tolerated when March rolled around and Miss Brown announced the production of the year. Sometimes it was a musical with orchestral help siphoned from the Louisville Junior Symphony. Other times it was a three-act: Aeschylus or Euripides, Ibsen or Oscar Wilde.

Since no boys attended LCD and the male staff consisted only of Mr. Pfeiffer in chemistry and Old Ben the janitor, Simone often found herself cast as a man. Her favorite role was senior year when they put on *Twelfth Night* and she played Viola, a woman pretending to be a man. The countess fell in love with her, she fell in love with the duke, and in the end she and her twin brother solved the problem by each marrying the opposite sex.

Besides drama, her other means of escape was riding horses. She was from Kentucky, after all. Her parents wouldn't listen to her pleas for a horse of her own so she had to settle for after school lessons on the worn out horses at LCD and Saturdays atop tall Tennessee walking horses at the Roan Stables not far from her house. Saturday mornings she dressed in breeches, ratcatcher shirt, and black hunt coat, and squeezed into high boots, strapped on spurs, grabbed her hard cap and crop, and dashed to the stables with a banana and a quarter for lunch.

After her lesson she practiced with the drill team, making formations in the ring, splitting into pairs, reconnecting as four, and forming figure eights to loud marching music. She loved the rhythm and the pure physical sensation of being jostled and carried by a huge, strong animal. She usually liked being part of the team, except for those awful days, the days when she'd been bad. She never knew what she'd done wrong, but she must have been bad because that's what the voice inside her head said: *You—are—stu—pid*, it repeated over and over in perfect timing with the horse's hooves. *You—are—ug—ly. No—one—likes—you*, it taunted as trumpets and timpani urged the horses on.

Where did this voice come from? She wanted to cry, to shout *Stop*, but when the voice spoke, the inside of her mouth changed. Her tongue became thick and dry as a desert. Ridges, like waves of sand, formed on the roof of her mouth. Her teeth were jagged stones and prickly cactus. Only when she got home, pulled off her manured boots, stripped out of her sweaty clothes, and stepped into a hot bath, could she exorcise the horrible feeling by sinking her whole body, head and all, under water.

The grandfather clock started to chime. Dinner would be ready. She scuffed into her pink satin high-heeled slippers and headed down the front stairs, careful not to trip on the silky edges of the kimono.

Chapter 14

VIOLET BLEW AT THE SPIRALS OF STRAY HAIR that hung loose in her face as she stood over the dishpan of sudsy water. Her mother had taught her to get a head start on cleaning up. Do the worst first, she always said. But Violet never seemed to get past the worst. She was forever cooking and cleaning and washing and ironing and keeping her mouth shut most of the day and night. She didn't have the leisurely life of Simone or the freedom to come and go like Randolph. She was stuck there twenty-four hours a day and worked from the first hint of dawn until the Milky Way speckled the sky and the North Star rose to its throne. Even her mother left the Applebaums when dinner dishes were done. All Violet could do to get away from the hornet's nest was go for a walk in the woods or down by the river. That's where she felt most at home, in the outdoors under the wide sky. But tonight the sky was encased by the storm, an icy cave where the only way out was blocked by a howling wind. It was if she were Elijah, waiting for the voice of God. But it's not in the wind, not in the earthquake, not even in the fire. He spoke in a still, small voice. That's what her mother told her. That's what the Bible said.

She wasn't sure about the voice of God, but she did remember the soft whisper of Earl Brown that night when she was fourteen, before he left for the army. They had never really talked until that night. She hadn't known he even noticed her. She thought she'd been the only one doing the watching—at church twice a week, across baseball fields, at the swimming creek, outside the Speckled Trout Grill. He was one of the older boys, smart as a beaver, graceful as a dogwood. But that night after the church picnic, he had walked her home and poured out his thoughts, one upon another like a golden stream, until she knew the shape of his heart as well as the shape of his hand. He pushed her in the tire swing under the willow tree near her house. His fingers were soft as willow leaves as they brushed the sides of her waist. When he pressed his lips on the nape of her neck, she felt like a Luna Moth bursting out of its casing, sprouting wings and ready to fly into the dark. He told her she was a star in his night sky and he would gaze at her forever, even from the other side of the earth. He twisted the swing, wound her up tight and high, then gave her a shove, and let her go. She spun wildly, legs and arms stretched wide into the night, as if she were the tide running up to meet the moon. She hung her head back and tried not to squeal. Earl's face, upside down and inky blue in the moonlight, was long and serious. His eyes drank her in. As she slowed, dizzy and dangly, he caught her, cocooned her head between his strong hands and kissed her eyelids. He was saying something but she couldn't hear; his hands covered her ears. His eyes were thick with tears. Then he left. Forever.

She knew she wouldn't be hearing any still, small voices tonight. From the looks of the snow building up on the window ledge over the kitchen sink, she wouldn't be going outside either. And from the sound of the duet that came from the piano earlier, Randolph had wriggled his way into Simone's graces. She had a feeling it wouldn't be easy to get either of them out of her hair tonight.

She bent over and put three dinner plates into the oven to warm—one gold-edged bone china plate with Mr. Blankwell's university chapel painted in blue, and two pottery plates, an orangey-red one for Randolph and a green one for her. She always picked that plate if she had a choice. It was the color of life, of leaves and grass. The color of the creek outside Willow Grove, the color of moss. It was new berries before they were ripe. Young peaches and even bananas. It was acorns and snapdragons and brand new trees. It was the color of all things before they were born, before they were spoiled. She stared over the sink into the black mirror of the window and imagined the Garden of Eden.

The wind moaned and beat so loudly on the mudroom door that she didn't hear the creak of the front staircase or the clicking of high heels in the passage outside the kitchen. She didn't notice someone enter the room, didn't even sense a presence until she saw a flash of iridescent blue reflected behind her in the window. It was as if she were outlined in turquoise, as if her spirit had seeped out and was glowing around her. She gave a start and spun around.

There was Simone in full regalia, wrapped in Mrs. Blankwell's prize kimono, a cigarette in a long ivory holder in one hand, a squat glass of bourbon in the other.

"Hope I didn't scare you," she said and took a sip of her drink. "Since it's just little ol' me at home tonight, I thought I'd have cocktails in here." She turned, showing the peacock design on the back of the robe. The eyes in the tail feathers blazed at Violet like a scene from the book of Revelation. "Hope you don't mind."

"No, Ma'am," Violet said and smoothed her hair into its roll. "Dinner's ready whenever you are."

Simone walked to the stove and leaned over the burners. "Smells yummy. I wish you'd teach me to cook sometime. One of these days Lincoln and I will be getting a house of our own and he'll expect me to feed him. By the way, did the phone ring while I was upstairs?"

"No, Ma'am. No calls." Then something made her add, "I'm sure you're a fine cook, Miss Simone." How did this girl make her lie?

"That's hardly how I would describe the few disasters I've fixed on my own. What cookbook do you use? *Joy of Cooking*?"

"That's what Mrs. Blankwell likes, but Ambra mostly cooks by the feel of it. It's not hard after you've made the same thing a few times. Ambra's the expert. You could ask her when she gets back."

Simone tottered across the room and flicked her ashes into the sink. "Filthy habit, isn't it?"

Violet began to mutter a compromising response but

Simone broke in. "Don't bother answering. I know you disapprove. You probably disapprove of my little cocktail, too. Is your daddy a preacher or something? One of those Bible thumpers in a shiny suit? Why'd he let you come up here, anyway? Doesn't he worry you'll be corrupted by these long-nosed Yankee money mongers?"

"My father's not a reverend," Violet started to say but Simone wasn't listening.

Simone drained her drink and dumped the ice cubes into the sink along with the butt of her cigarette. "Enough of this. I'll have a glass of wine with dinner. You think I can trust old Randolph to choose a good bottle from the cellar? Where is he anyway? *Randolph*," she called. "Did he go back to his rooms?" She peered out the kitchen window. "I wonder what they're like. Have you ever been up there?" She turned to Violet and winked. "I must confess, I've peeked in his windows—once or twice—but don't tell." She held her finger to her lips. "Oh, what the hell, I shouldn't be admitting this to you, but one time I even sneaked in."

"I'm sure he's still in the house," Violet said. "The storm's too wild right now for anyone to go outside."

"Well then, where's he hiding? Under your skirt?" Simone bent low, wobbly on her pink high heels. "*Randolph*," she called again, this time louder. "Come out, come out, wherever you are."

Simone's loose tongue was frightening, blowing recklessly like the wind outside. "Would you like me to serve your dinner now?" Violet tried to calm her. "The table in the dining room is set." She'd never seen this giddy side of Simone before. She'd seen her laugh, especially when Lincoln's friends were over. She'd heard her yell and even scream upstairs in her room, usually at Lincoln, but sometimes even when she was alone. But this little-girl play-acting was something new.

"Of course you've got my place set. Silver and crystal for one. But I see you've got *two* places laid out here in the kitchen. You and Randolph. How cozy." Simone ran her fingers across the yellow and white checked tablecloth on the kitchen table. "It's so drafty out there in the dining room. Cold and lonely, and a little bit scary, don't you think?" Her mood was jumping up and down. One minute she was haughty and mean, the next she was whimpering. "Of course, you *like* to be alone, don't you? I've seen you wandering out there by the cedars." She pointed to the back window. "And I've seen you heading off to the river, too." She swung her arm in the other direction. "There's a lot I can see from my bedroom windows. But you know that, don't you?"

Violet trembled. Had Simone seen her in the window that afternoon?

"*Randolph!*" Simone yelled again at the top of her voice, and before she could take another breath he appeared around the corner.

"*Mon Dieu*, woman," he said with a laugh. "Is the house on fire, or only you?" He saw that her spirits had elevated since their piano duet. Maybe his touch on her ankle had flipped the switch.

Violet busied herself with mashed potatoes.

"There you are, you bushy-haired Druid." She stuck her thin arms into the wide sleeves of the kimono and hugged herself, bobbling side to side.

"I see you've embraced the true Blankwell identity." He

pointed to her robe. He wanted to tell her that a group of peacocks was called an ostentation.

"I've been a Blankwell for seven months now, thank you. Aren't I entitled to raid the treasure chest once in awhile?"

"Here, here," he said pretending to raise a toast. "You go ahead and do whatever you want. Isn't that what makes life sing?"

"And speaking of treasures," she smiled at him, "would you do me a teentsie-weentsie favor and run down into the cellar and fetch me a bottle of wine? Something old and fruity and full-bodied, something strong enough for a storm like tonight."

"Certainly Simone," he said, but his eyes met Violet's, who raised her brows. He saluted Simone and walked across the room to the basement door. As he started down the stairs he poked his head back into the room. "Only one?"

"Oh, bring two, and maybe I'll let you have a nip. That is, if you and Violet would care to share your table with me. Break bread together and all that. Let bygones be bygones."

Violet huffed. What bygones? But she knew if she were patient, Simone's secrets would reveal themselves.

"I heard that scorn, Miss Priss," Simone said staring at Violet. "Can't we all be friends, if only for one night?"

"Certainly Ma'am. You can eat wherever you like." She went to get another set of flatware and a napkin from the drawer.

"And enough of this Ma'am business. Call me Simone."

"Yes, Simone." The word felt slippery and sad. "Would you prefer your regular dinner plate, or a colored one like ours?" She brought the three warm plates from the oven.

"Not that chapel plate from Lincoln's university—as if he or his father ever set foot in that building. They're ardent atheists. No, give me the green one. It matches my robe."

Everything for the princess.

"Ah ha!" Randolph burst up the stairs holding a bottle in each hand. A cobweb clung to one end of his mustache. "This should fit the bill: Pinot Noir from the Côte d'Or. The bottles are dusty enough. I found them in a back corner. I thought we needed red on a night like tonight. After all, it is the Ides of March."

Simone clapped her hands. "Spectacular! I'll go find some glasses. This will be fun. When the cat's away, the mice will play." She teetered out into the pantry, her heels clicking.

Randolph set the bottles by the sink. "Better wipe these off," he told Violet. "She's in rare form tonight."

Violet spooned potatoes and peas onto the plates and set a platter of fried chicken in the center of the table. "Might as well do family style," she said under her breath.

"Cheer up, chum." Randolph lifted her chin with his finger. "You're still number one with me."

She snapped at his finger with her teeth. He infuriated her. Always teasing. She was wary of him like a wild dog. But at the same time she wanted to bury her face in his fur.

Chapter 15

THE OLD FARMHOUSE WAS HOME to a number of furs. Mrs. Blankwell had two full-length mink coats: a brown wild mink with deep magenta satin lining that had been her mother's, and a snazzy silver-gray ranch-raised one, lined in baby-blue, that Mr. Blankwell had bought her on the occasion of his early retirement at age fifty. She also had a boa of five brown minks, heads with glass eyes and feet with sharp nails, all biting one another's tails. Mr. Blankwell had a raccoon coat left over from his college years, but it rarely left the cedar closet. Lincoln had a hat made of reindeer skin that his mother brought back from Helsinki. That stayed in the cedar closet, too.

When Simone turned sixteen her mother had given her the choice between two winter coats: a beaver or a leopard. Beaver, like mink or raccoon or even reindeer, would compliment any outfit, blending well in the woods and towns of North America. But leopard? Who expected to meet that giant jungle peacock-eater at the front door of a well-groomed suburban home in Louisville, Kentucky?

Spots offered camouflage in Kenya, but in the Midwest they roared "Look at me!" Simone chose leopard.

Lincoln was ambivalent to Simone's Old World fur. Some days it made him dizzy with delight. It announced that he was married to a wild woman. But other days, and especially the nights when they went out with the Spooks, he resented her attention-getting flamboyance. Putting on the leopard felt tantamount to taking off her wedding ring. It made her hold her head a little too high, her stance a little too wide. She had a horrible habit of rubbing her cheek against the collar. He was afraid she might start purring.

It wasn't just Simone's leopard coat that raised ambivalence in Lincoln. He loved her. She was gorgeous. She was playful. She was well bred with just enough artistic temperament thrown in to make her stand above the crowd. But that was the key word: above. Sometimes she crossed over that line and stood apart from the crowd, away from the way he liked to have things done. During their brief courtship he hadn't realized that she wasn't a joiner. All he had been interested in was her long bones, her smooth skin, her velvet, feverish lips. But now they were married and he was on his way up. They were going places. Didn't she know he needed her to fit in? Sometimes she seemed more like a kid sister—or a bratty girl from the neighborhood—than his wife. If he could look inside that pretty head, he was sure he'd see a solid streak of rebellion running right though the middle. Hadn't she put up a silly fuss on their honeymoon when he told her to hide three fifths of Scotch in her straw bag when they went through customs in Acapulco? And whenever he made a suggestion—like why don't you join the garden club or take cooking classes—she automatically dismissed him as if he didn't have her best interests at heart. Even when he tried to praise her—like the time she won second prize for her watercolor at the Women's City Club—she got furious with him when he asked why she didn't win first. He tried to tell her that defiance was unbecoming, and that insubordination would only hurt her in the end, but she pouted and cried and threw her bath oil at him, saying he thought she was stupid and ugly.

Well, if the truth be known, an unsubmissive wife was an ugly thing. Whereas a submissive woman—like that girl Violet—knew how to act in public. He bet a hundred bucks that public submissiveness made her even more fun in private. He hadn't tested his theory with the maid, but he was pretty sure that the calm reserve she showed on duty only fed her need to express her passion in private. That rogue Randolph was probably reaping the benefits on a regular basis. Lincoln pointed his theory out to Simone one night after she'd worn herself ragged in one of her fits. "Walk the line during the day so you can step over it at night," he told her. Instead of thanks, he got nicked with a flying hairbrush. That's when he knew for sure that he needed to get out of his parents' house and into a place of his own.

Hence his business trip in March. Simone didn't know it, but he was carving out a territory for himself with the help of his old chum Ginny. Her husband was already a bank vice president in Chicago. There was nothing like an old friend to give you a foot up in the world. If all went as planned, by June they would be on their way to a cute Cape Cod in a quiet suburb on the north shore of Chicago.

Maybe Simone and her leopard skin would blend in better in the Windy City.

Then it would be babies for her and racquetball after work for him. She could take art classes and cooking and spend summers at the lake with his mother. That would do the trick—a few months one-on-one with his mother and Simone would know how to behave. The other girls at the lake would fill her in. She'd do just fine. He could visit on weekends. Besides she looked great in a swimsuit.

After a thorough inspection, and a bit of forethought,
the house mover disconnects, seals, and caps the utilities:
electricity, plumbing, heating.

Chapter 16

SIMONE TIPTOED BAREFOOT into the kitchen with three wineglasses and a corkscrew dangling from her fingers, humming Cole Porter's "Night and Day." The kimono had slipped low on one shoulder and her hair, always a mess of curls, sprung from head like Spanish moss.

"I have the most wonderful idea!" she said, as if Violet and Randolph were suddenly her new best friends. "Let's play a game after dinner."

"What do you have in mind?" Randolph asked and leaned back in his chair at the head of the table. He was already biting into a steaming chicken breast.

"Show some manners, Randolph," Violet hissed and nudged his chair back onto four legs. "Wait until we say grace."

"Oh, I don't know," Simone said. "Scrabble, Clue, Chinese Checkers?" She sat down at the place with the green plate.

"Poker, Gin, Spin the Bottle?" Randolph said and hummed the next line of Cole Porter where Simone had left off.

"None of that." Violet shot him a stern look and sat down at the table opposite Simone. How odd to be sitting knee to knee with her highness. Why would Simone want to eat in the kitchen anyway? Was she just a lonely girl or did she have something else in mind for the evening? Something more than a game?

"Are you going to say a blessing?" Simone carefully arranged her folded hands to best capture the light in her huge engagement diamond.

"Of course she will," Randolph said. "Violet loves to pray."

Violet lowered her head and closed her eyes. She was tired of Randolph's teasing. He thought he could play her up and down like a piano, sometimes loud, sometimes soft, but always moving, fingering her body and now her soul. She hurried through a few words of thanksgiving.

At the *Amen* Simone said, "How sweet. How utterly sweet and innocent. Mrs. Blankwell always recites a line out of the *Book of Common Prayer*. You speak as if some-one is listening."

Violet handed Simone the platter of chicken. Why pray if you didn't think anyone was listening? she thought.

They ate in awkward silence as snow pelted the windows.

"So," Simone said to Randolph, "you enjoy Cole Porter?"

"Naturally," he said, and sang "*This longing for you follows me wherever I go.*" He slid his eyes over her bare shoulder then paused to draw a blush. "I like Nat King Cole, too." He winked at Violet.

Simone drew the kimono closer, enjoying his attention. "Please pass *The Frim Fram Sauce*." She showed off her knowledge of Nat King Cole as she pointed to the gravy boat.

Randolph guffawed. She was up on her music. Old Lincoln must be giving her lessons. "You know that naughty song's been banned by NBC," he said handing her the gravy.

"Well, I listen to it on WWJ from Detroit." She ladled gravy on her potatoes. "Say, why don't we turn on the radio right now? Have a little mood music with our dinner. Violet, go get the Philco from the library. I'll pour the wine and we'll have ourselves a party."

Violet slid from her chair.

"It's heavy; I'll help." Randolph started to get up from the table but Simone laid a hand across his arm.

"Surely she can manage," she said with a pout. "I need a strong man to unscrew this cork."

Violet rolled her eyes and left the room.

Simone fumbled with the tinfoil covering the cork, then inserted the screw like an expert.

"Looks like you've got that covered," Randolph said.

"I might have done this once or twice before." She pushed her chair out from the table and held the bottle between her legs. "But I could use some assistance now." She smiled up at him. "I wouldn't want the whole thing to spill in my lap."

Randolph got up and stood behind her, putting his

hand over hers as they turned the screw together. Her hair smelled like almonds.

"Now I'll press down this lever." She moved her hand from under his. "And *voila*." The wine made a quiet exhaling sound, like a genie coming out of a lamp. At the same time there was a loud rumble outdoors, then a crack and a flash. "Lightning," said Simone.

"Thunder," said Randolph.

As Violet returned carrying the unwieldy radio box she saw Randolph bent over Simone.

He stood quickly and took the big wooden radio from her arms. Just then the overhead light flickered and went out. The house was in darkness. "So much for the radio," he said.

"Ooh," Simone said and clapped her hands. "How exciting."

In a moment a match flared in Randolph's fingers. Violet was already holding a candle. "Let's calm down and finish our dinner before everything gets cold," she said and set two more candles on the table for Randolph to light. They took their places again and Simone filled her wineglass with the Pinot Noir.

"Sounds like rain," Simone said and took a deep drink. Drops of water were hitting the panes from the east and immediately turning to ice. The rumbling continued. "This is so odd," she said. "Snow and then rain—and then ice."

"It's the middle of March," Violet said. "They say in like a lion and out like a lamb. Maybe we're at the turning point."

"The Ides of March," Randolph said.

"When Druids read their fortunes in chicken bones,

right?" Simone giggled and held up what was left of a wing and a thigh. "Tell me what you see."

"Great idea," he said. "Let's all put our bones on the table. You, too, Violet."

"But that's divination," she said.

"What's the matter, you afraid of Mr. Bayou's voodoo?" Simone said. "I thought all you pick-a-ninnies loved that sort of thing."

"Simone!" Randolph growled.

"Sorry," she said and gave Violet a blank look. "I was just being funny. Just trying to loosen up Miss Bible Bones." She held up the wine bottle. "Here you two, have some." She filled their glasses.

"I'll start with my future," Randolph said, "to show you there's nothing to be afraid of. Though it doesn't always work to read your own. Too many presumptions and mixed messages. But I'll give it a try." He took the bones from the breast and drumstick he'd eaten, held them lightly in his fingers, then let them drop onto the tablecloth in front of his plate. The candlelight made flickering shadows. "*Hmmm.*" He closed his eyes and let his hands hover above the pile. "I haven't done this in awhile. And my mother always used a whole carcass—duck or quail."

"My mother would shiver in her bones if she knew I was sitting here watching this," Violet said. She fingered the edge of her wineglass and the crystal began to hum.

"Perfect," said Simone, "a little mood music." She licked her finger and rubbed her glass. It made a higher sound since it was nearly empty. The kitchen flashed white as another stroke of lightning filled the sky. A loud clap of thunder followed close behind.

"The storm's nearly on top of us," Violet said.

"That's the spirits," Randolph said, his eyes still closed. "The bones are starting to talk."

"What do they say?" Simone poured more wine into her glass. "Romance? Betrayal? Murder?"

Randolph opened his eyes and spread his hands to make a frame above the bones. "I see movement, travel. Maybe a sudden trip. I see a dark path or a river and something that looks like a broken bridge. Bits and pieces that look like splinters. Damn. I hope that's not a broken finger." He moved his hands away quickly and knocked over his wineglass. "Oops," he said.

"Don't worry. The glass didn't break," Simone said. "And there's another bottle right over there."

"I was thinking of the tablecloth," he said. Violet started moving dishes and mopping up the spill with a dishcloth.

"Leave that until later," Simone said. "I want my future read." She jiggled her bones and tossed them in the air like a pair of dice and let them drop in front of her. "Study them, Randy, while I uncork the next bottle."

"I'll see to the shortcake," Violet said and pushed away from the table, away from their dangerous game, and began clearing the dishes. She carried her untouched wineglass to the sink and set it on the windowsill, out of reach—and temptation. She'd never been drunk, and if it made people act as ugly as Simone—calling her a pick-a-ninny—she didn't want any part of it.

"I don't know, Simone." Randolph shook his head as he stared at the bones. "Are you sure you want to hear what I see?"

"Of course. This *hocus pocus* adds a whole new dimension to life."

"You mean *Hoc est corpus meum*," Randolph said. " 'This is my body.' "

"Like from the Mass?" Simone said. "Are you saying magic's really a Catholic thing? Turning water into wine and wine into blood and all that?"

"Not exactly, Simone." Randolph marveled at her naïveté.

"So go on, tell me what you see."

He sighed. "There's definitely something here. A pond? A pool? It's small and round. I see water—or something darker. I'm not sure what it is."

"Maybe my bathtub upstairs. That's where I'm headed when this little soirée is over tonight."

"That could be it because now I see something lying in the water, or whatever it is. Something small and white that looks like it's floating away."

A shiver ran through Simone. How could he know? No one knew. Not even Lincoln. "Oh, that's me," she said, "adrift in mounds of bubbles. Now it's Violet's turn."

"No," Violet said from the counter where she was spooning whipped cream over the strawberries.

"I insist," Simone said. "We're all in this together. Bring your bones over here right now." Her voice rose to a command. "Let's find out the truth about you. What secrets are *you* hiding?"

Violet set two plates of dessert on the table. "I don't want to," she said. "Besides, I don't have any secrets."

"Really?" Randolph said.

Violet didn't answer.

"You're just a fraidy cat," Simone said

"It's dangerous to tempt the spirit world," Violet said.

"I think she's afraid we'll find out her secret desires, don't you, Randolph?"

"Or *who* she desires," he said

The two of them started singing, "*Who she's dreaming of night and day?*" while Simone got up from the table and retrieved what was left of Violet's breast and chicken wing. "Here Randolph," she said handing the bones to him. "Tell Violet what she wants to hear."

"It doesn't work like that," he said. "I can't just say I see prince charming and a beautiful castle, even if I know that's what she's waiting for."

"Don't you mean a handsome Zulu warrior and a fancy grass hut?"

Violet clenched her teeth. She felt wickedness creeping out of the darkness, flaring up at her like the shadows cast by the candles on the table.

"Or maybe she has a mysterious dark man waiting for her back home?" Simone winked at Randolph. "Or a secret lover she meets in the woods—or could it be the garage?"

Randolph stretched out his palms to Violet: "Baby, you know I'm yours for the taking."

Violet could hold her anger in no longer. She slapped his face.

Randolph rubbed his cheek and laughed. "I like my women hot."

"My, my," said Simone. She was still standing by the table. "A lover's quarrel?"

"Be quiet," Violet said, spinning around to look at Simone.

"Now the truth comes out," Simone said.

"Stop talking," she said again, cradling the hand that still stung from the slap.

"So this is what you're up to, *night and day.*" Simone sang the phrase in her drunken little-girl voice.

Violet felt trapped, and before she could bite her tongue her thoughts escaped: "Shut up you bitch!"

"Bitch?" Simone laughed in a wobbly voice. "How dare you, you snooty nigger, you black-skinned whore!" She rose to her full height. "You always act so high and mighty. Poor little Cinderella. You think you deserve a fairy godmother. Well, I've got news for you. She's not coming. And I thought I was being nice to you, eating with you in the kitchen, sharing my wine." She swept her hand toward the table in a gesture of largess. "But now I see the truth. I'm spoiling your little tête-à-tête with Randolph. I'm cramping your style." She circled the table and leaned her face right into Violet's. "I hate to be the one to tell you, but you're the odd one out, not me." She poked Violet between the breasts. "You're the one who's bred from savages, whose grandparents were slaves. You're the one with a half-wit twin sister who should have been drowned at birth—like a deformed kitten: Rosie the Retard." Simone chanted the words in a sing-songy voice and wiggled her fingers next to her ears. "Rosie the Retard, Rosie the Retard."

Violet could stand the taunting no more. How dare this drunken woman insult her dearest Rosie. She lifted her plate of strawberry short cake and smacked it right into Simone's face, then turned on her heels and fled to her room.

"Oh my God," screamed Simone, wiping her face with

the edge of the already soiled tablecloth. "You'll pay for this!"

Randolph tried to bite back his laughter.

"What are you smirking about?" she shouted at Randolph, and ran barefoot up the back stairs.

Chapter 17

VIOLET SAT IN HER DARK ROOM, full of shame. Emotions roiled around her like the storm outside, pelting her with shards of icy guilt. Who was she turning into? She acted so out of character—slapping Randolph, swearing at Simone, throwing that plate of food in her face. She'd shocked them both, and herself as well. Her heart still throbbed and her face was burning hot. She lay down on her bed and tried to take slow, steady breaths. Mama's words rose up in a vision over her bed. *Keep the engineer of right thinking out front; don't get pulled backwards by the caboose of feelings.* She could almost see the train. But what made her act so impulsively? Randolph's insinuation that she was attracted to him? How dare he accuse her of lust? But as soon as she named that word, *lust,* she felt the tug of her conscience and started to cry again. How pitiful I am, she moaned and rolled over, to even think a white man and a colored girl, a Christian and an occultist…to even harbor the idea…and he's such a brute! She would put her fantasies behind her; he would not cajole her again.

She calmed herself down and sat on the edge of the bed. Water was running in the kitchen sink and upstairs in the tub. Why did she let Simone get under her skin? That girl had everything presented to her on a silver platter and never did a thing to help other people. She just moped around the house one day like a poor pathetic dog, then flitted around like a drunken butterfly the next. What right did she have to say such horrible things? Simone's sing-songy voice assaulted her again: *Rosie the Retard, Rosie the Retard.* The refrain wound its way into the dark corner of her heart where guilt over Rosie's birth lay like a stone. She willed the voice to stop. She had to take control of herself. No matter how many times she thought it—or how true it was—Violet should never have let that word slip out of her mouth, especially at Simone. And what possessed her to push that plate into her face? She was as big a fool as that stupid, drunken girl. Now she would pay. She would be fired tomorrow, or whenever Lincoln got home. Simone would tell him about everything and that would be the end of that. And she deserved it. It was her fault. She lost control. Simone won. She buried her face in her pillow again and cried.

Simone groped her way up the dark staircase and down the hall to her room. She used the wide arms of the kimono to wipe off the rest of the strawberries and cream, then dropped it on the chaise, shedding her bra and panties on her way to the bathroom. She could draw her bath blind-folded. She lined up her assortment of candles on the vanity and lit them. They gave off a soft glow.

The confrontation with Violet was a catharsis for

Simone. Venting always helped her ride her feelings over the top and into a calmer, duller emotional state. She was surprised at that girl; she would never have guessed Violet had so much spunk. It was fun, actually, to meet her match. At school the other girls had been afraid of her theatrics. She liked to think her petty quarrels provided an avenue for testing and strengthening relationships, rather than a way to destroy them, though most of her friends claimed she was cruel. They just didn't understand her. Not one of them would have dared to throw a plate of food in her face.

When the tub was full, she stepped into the hot water, bubbles coating the surface like frosting. She sank below the froth until the water was up to her chin. The effects of the wine and alcohol were wearing off. As the water relaxed her body, her mind unwound too. She drifted back to Randolph's fortune telling. She wanted to believe that what he had seen was just this: her taking a bath. But she wasn't floating away. She couldn't fool herself that much. And the fluttering down in her belly didn't lie. A wave of sadness overcame her. She didn't want to think about it and she certainly didn't want to cry.

She stood in the tub and leaned toward the medicine chest, reaching a dripping arm over the candles and into the corner of the top shelf. Hidden behind the Noxema jar she found a bottle of pills left over from her pre-wedding jitters. She wasn't sure what the doctor had prescribed, but it always made her feel good. She hoarded the pills, only letting herself have one in an emergency. But surely surviving this snowstorm all alone entitled her to a little extra help. As she popped one of the pills into her mouth and swallowed it dry, she noticed the lights in her bedroom came back on.

When the lights suddenly came back on, Violet sat up in her bed and dried her eyes on her apron. Was it a sign? Maybe it wasn't too late to apologize. Maybe Simone would have pity on her. Or maybe she was too drunk to remember. She had to try to make amends.

O God, help me, she whispered as she crept out of her room and down the narrow hallway to the servants' stairs. She could see Randolph with his back to her clearing the mess from the table. Quickly she climbed the stairs, avoiding the steps that creaked. She had done this a hundred times before. She could move like a shadow through the house.

She walked silently to Simone's open door and went in. The kimono lay on the chaise; Simone's underwear was on the floor. She must be in the tub. She whispered another prayer, then knocked gently at the door.

"Miss Simone?" she said in her most submissive voice.

There was only the sound of splashing.

"Miss Simone?" she said a little louder.

"What? Is that you, you little animal?"

"I am so sorry."

"I guess you should be. Who do you think you are, anyway?"

"I forgot, Miss Simone. I lost my head. I know I don't deserve to be forgiven."

"You deserve to be terminated tonight, that's what you deserve."

"Yes, Ma'am, I do. And I'll go now if that's what you want."

"Oh cut the martyr act. You can't go out in this storm. Besides, fighting with you was the most fun I've had in a long time. Violet, I didn't know you could swear. Did you see the look on Randolph's face? He was as red as his mustache—and speechless. That was worth a little strawberry shortcake."

Violet couldn't believe her ears. This was too good to be true.

"And you made sure my fortune came true—here I am in the tub."

"Can I do anything for you?" Violet asked.

"I left my cigarettes out there in the bedroom. Bring me the pack, and my lighter too."

Violet got them off the side table and went back to the bathroom. She opened the door a crack. A row of candles burned along the edge of the vanity giving off a strong scent of jasmine. Simone's thin white ankles were crossed and resting on the side of the tub. The bottoms of her toes were stained dark orange from her wet loafers. Violet would have to scrub and scrub to get the oxblood stain out of her socks.

"Here they are, Ma'am."

"I thought I told you not to call me Ma'am. You make me sound like my mother-in-law, God forbid." She reached in the direction of the door and Violet dropped the cigarettes and lighter into her hand. "Now shut the door; there's a draft. And take a look at the kimono would you? It will probably have to go to the dry cleaners."

"I'll see to it."

"One more thing. I hope there'll be a fresh plate of dessert waiting for me when I get out of the tub."

"Certainly, Simone. There will be."

Randolph listened to the slam of Simone's bedroom door and thought, "That's why I'm a bachelor. Women are crazy." Over in France during the war they called women "field mattresses." Comfortable to be with at night, but not much use in the day. Way too heavy to lug around. Even at night they couldn't be trusted. He remembered one mademoiselle. Never knew her name, and was glad for that now. Less details to haunt him. She almost had him fooled, curling up with him night after night in the stone pigeon house where he slept, then waking him before dawn with her French tricks. He was starting to like it, starting to like her. Until the morning he woke with a gun to his head. He was well-trained and his reflexes were fast. A scissor grip with his legs, and in an instant her neck was throbbing under his hands as she stared at him with her collaborator eyes. Finally she went lax and he let go. It was hideous how her beautiful face turned into a horror, but that was war. A man did what he had to do.

He went to the sink and splashed cold water in his face. Thank God that the war was over. But another, much tamer one, was brewing in the house tonight. He'd always known Simone was a grenade with a loose pin, but the fury that erupted from Violet surprised him. She was volcanic. He hadn't even know she had a sister.

Or was her wrath really aimed at him? With all the words that flew like cat fur, he'd almost forgotten her slap.

He could still feel the slight burn of her hand against his cheek. Maybe she had a sweet spot for him after all. And what about Simone? She actually sounded like she was jealous. Maybe they were fighting over him. Fancy that. Women were a conundrum. They purred and preened, then spread their claws and hissed. A tiger had risen up in Violet and smashed that strawberry shortcake right up Simone's haughty feline nose. A regular cat fight. This would be a night to remember.

Just then the lights came on. He surveyed the kitchen: wine spilled on the tablecloth, strawberry shortcake on the floor, and chicken bones all over the place. It was odd how divination—as Violet called it—always ended in chaos. But at least the lights were back on. He could plug in the radio and do up the dishes. Maybe the women would cool down and he could have more fun later.

He fiddled with the tuning knob; the storm was creating static on the airwaves. Then he caught the blood-chilling strains of Stravinsky's *The Rite of Spring*. Could anything be more perfect on a night like this? A full glass of wine stood on the windowsill. It would be a sin to let something so good go to waste. He guzzled it down and sighed as the acrid heat spread down into his belly. He filled the sink with hot sudsy water and let the music run up and down his backbone. The window in front of him was opaque with frozen rain and snow that sealed them in like a tomb.

Chapter 18

VIOLET CLOSED SIMONE'S BEDROOM DOOR and shook her head. Was this a dream? How could that girl go from hot to cold and back again so fast? She picked up the kimono and checked to see if the strawberries and whipped cream had spilled down its front. It was hard to tell with all the ornate patterns. The gown felt heavenly, light as a feather. She loved its color, shiny and iridescent like a rainbow trout. She couldn't resist. She slipped it on over her uniform, picked up the dark red sash and tied it around her waist. She stretched her arms and admired the long, flowing sleeves. She felt regal.

She went out in the hall, standing rim rod straight, and walked slowly, pointing one foot in front of the other. She twirled on her tiptoes, her head held high. Everything was going to be fine. She knew she should hang the kimono up in Mrs. B's dressing room and take a closer look at it in the morning, but she couldn't pass up admiring her reflection in the big bay window at the top of the stairs; she had to stop. It was the same the spot where she had first seen the storm coming across the river earlier in the day. Even though it was dark in the hall, she could still make out her turquoise shape in the ice-coated window. She rippled her arms up and down like a shimmer of willow leaves caught in a breeze.

The bottom step of the big staircase gave out a telltale groan. Randolph was coming upstairs. She had no time so she stepped to the side of the window and turned toward the curtain, hoping she would blend in. She tried to slow her breathing. He mounted the first landing, humming that awful "Night and Day" song again. *In the silence of my lonely room, under the high moon.* He was at the top. He hesitated. Where was he going, anyway?

He approached the window seat and leaned toward the glass. She kept her eyes lowered and peeked at him from the side. Randolph had his hands flat against the panes. She'd have to wash his smudges off tomorrow. Now he was breathing into the window, fogging it up with his hot breath. He pressed his lips against the glass. What things people did when they thought they were alone.

Then she sensed it. He had spotted her. She could feel him looking right at her. She kept her face to the curtain, wondering what he would say. But he was silent. She heard him move toward her.

"There you are," he whispered. "I came to see if you were all right." He was close behind her now. "You look so delicious in this peacock robe." He slipped his arms around her waist, drew her back against his body. She stiffened.

"You just need a little love, a little tenderness." She could smell the wine on his breath. "You must be awfully lonely." He pressed his nose into her hair, then laughed and pushed her away. "Violet, you tart!"

"Shush," she said. "She's in the tub."

"And you're in her dress."

"And you thought you were fingering the master's wife, you two-timing eel." That's not what she meant to say. Two-timing whom? He disgusted her, didn't he?

"Oh no, Violet, you've got it all wrong." He back-pedaled. "I knew it was you. Aren't you the one who needs some loving?"

"Liar. I saw you with her in the kitchen, your nose in her long silky hair."

"That's not how it was. She called me over. She needed help with the wine bottle." Sounds like jealousy to me, thought Randolph.

"You can't weasel out of it."

A door down the hall opened and shut. "You'd better weasel out of that kimono," he said. "And fast. She's coming."

Violet slipped off the robe and ran into Mrs. Blankwell's room. Randolph sped down the stairs, three at a time. And after a few moments Simone sauntered along the hall, a thick terry cloth robe around her body and a towel twisted Cleopatra-style around her head.

Chapter 19

A PROGRESSION OF DARK, MELANCHOLY CHORDS sounded from the piano as Simone swept down the stairs bundled in her bathrobe, a thick pair of Lincoln's socks on her feet. "That's lovely," she said standing behind Randolph. "What is it?"

"A little something I'm working on. Glad to see you've recovered."

"Wasn't that a scene in the kitchen? I should have known better than to tangle with that girl. Besides, wine always goes to my head. Not to mention the storm outside. It's driving me crazy. And I'm worried about Lincoln—the phone didn't ring while I was in the tub did it?"

"Not that I heard." He kept playing.

"Violet came up and apologized, so now I'm off to get another plate of dessert from her. This time I'll feed myself." She gave him a smile and turned toward the kitchen. He had to think fast. Violet was still upstairs.

"You could do me a favor," he said.

"Yes?"

"I'm working on a duet and I could use two more hands."

"Oh, well you know I'm not very good."

"You're good enough."

"But it's awfully chilly out here. Could we do it later?" She hugged her robe around her shoulders. "Or better yet, would you mind lighting the fire while I get my dessert?"

He heard clinking sounds from the direction of the kitchen. "My pleasure," he said jumping up.

"I'll bring out my dessert and get comfy. Then you can serenade me with your music." She turned and went to the kitchen.

At the fireplace he opened the damper and struck a match to the already laid fire. Wind howled in the chimney but the draft drew the smoke up and out of the house leaving barely a scent. He walked the few steps into the sunroom. Its windows faced in three directions and all of them were covered with ice. From what he could see, the rain had turned back to snow. This was the strangest storm he'd ever heard of. The wind was so wild there were tall drifts on every side of the house. He wouldn't be surprised if all the doors and windows were iced over and frozen shut. He might not be able to get to his rooms over the garage. He might just have to spend the night in the house with the girls.

The fire burned hot and bright and the pinecones he always threw in par Mrs. B's request crackled and glowed. The brass bucket was full of wood and he'd stacked more dry logs on the screened-in porch. They could keep warm for a week. He sat down in Mr. B's chair. He was beginning to feel quite at home in it. He pulled out his pipe and pouch of tobacco, and with his feet up on the ottoman he breathed a sigh of relief. The cats were purring again.

"Aren't you crafty," Simone said as she slid into the chair opposite Randolph and balanced a plate of strawberry short cake on her lap. The diamond rings on both her hands glittered in the firelight.

"There's not much to lighting a fire when the elements are ready."

"When I was a girl back in Louisville I used to creep out of the house every afternoon when my mother took a nap," Simone crossed her ankles and wiggled her toes in her heavy socks, "I'd run barefoot through the blackberry brambles to a bit of hardscrabble around an old foundation where our cook's two boys used to pitch clay marbles in the dirt." She took the wet towel off her head and fingered her hair, dangling it before the fire. "Sometimes I'd sneak bits of food—sausages and bread mainly—and we'd roast them on sticks. When my mother woke up she'd clang the bell and I'd run home, knowing I was in for a whipping. She forbid me to play with scabberbaggers."

"Scabberbaggers?"

"Whatever she meant, it was bad. But those boys were my friends. They were great at fire building. I could never get the wood to catch."

"Maybe you were smothering it. There has to be a channel for the air to draw through the fuel. Fire chases air through wood."

"Or though leaves—like your pipe. My Daddy smoked a pipe. I love the aroma." Back in Louisville her father always had a pipe in his mouth, a finger of bourbon on his desk, and a half grin on his face. "He called me 'Babykins' and gave me an honorary seat on the leather foot stool in his study where he was forever reading the *St Louis Post-Dispatch* and answering his mail. I would sit cross-legged and run my fingers across the cool hard bumps of the brass tacks on its side. Sometimes he'd let me slit open his lawyer letters with the brass knife he kept in his top drawer. Maybe that's why I like the study in the house so much—it reminds me of him."

"Ever smoked one of these yourself?" he asked, nodding to his pipe.

"Are you kidding? Lincoln thinks cigarettes are disgusting."

Randolph took his pipe from his mouth and moved forward onto the ottoman, turning the shank around and holding it out to her. "Care to try mine, Babykins?"

"Don't mind if I do," she said and slipped the bit into her mouth. She sucked in, then coughed. "Aach!"

"You're not supposed to breathe in fast; just tease the smoke into your mouth, then let it drift away."

She tried again. "Like this?" She drew on the pipe and let the smoke puff out the side of her mouth.

"Perfect," he said. They sat in silence as the air grew heavy with the scent of tobacco. The fire hissed and burned. Wind rousted the windowpanes. The grandfather clock began to strike. "Nine already?" Simone said. "So late and Lincoln hasn't called."

"Maybe the phone's out. I heard a news bulletin on the radio. This is the worst storm in thirty years."

"I didn't think of that," she said and handed him the pipe. "I'll go see if I can reach the operator."

She crossed the living room, walked around the piano and into the hall. The telephone resided in its own separate closet behind the stairs, with a bench along one wall wide enough for two. The door had a small Tiffany-type stained glass window, so from inside you could see shapes passing when the door was shut, but no one could see into the tiny room unless the overhead light was pulled on. She picked up the receiver and tapped the lever in the cradle. No operator; the line was dead. Maybe Lincoln had been trying to call, like he promised. Maybe her suspicions were just her imagination and he was on an innocent business trip. She wished she had checked the phone earlier. Then she would know for sure when his alibi began.

She was about to open the closet door when Violet's shadow passed by, moving in the direction of the living room. Was she going to join Randolph? Simone would love to overhear their conversation. She crept out of the telephone room, circled behind the staircase, and tiptoed through the front hall. The padded bench outside the powder room door was deep in shadows and a perfect place to hide.

Violet walked up to the back of the chair where Simone had been sitting and glared at Randolph. "I see you're making yourself at home—in someone else's house."

"I live here, Violet, just like you do."

"Not exactly. You and I, we work here. I don't call that living."

"All work and no play makes Jack a dull boy."

"You play plenty. Isn't that what your work is? Playing?"

"Have a seat, Violet. Tonight is different. Even the

heavens are telling you that. Snow changing to rain. Ice covering snow. It's just the three of us. Can't we relax and have fun?"

"Looks like you've been working on fun already." She walked over to the ottoman and picked up Simone's dirty plate. "You been sharing her strawberries too?"

Simone scowled in her hiding place. She remembered Randolph's joke at the piano before dinner about tasting strawberries with Violet in the kitchen.

"You're not jealous, are you?" he said.

"Don't flatter yourself. I'm just worried for you and the trouble you're aimed straight into. An uprooted plant is at the mercy of the wind."

"Is that some Bible verse?"

She shook her head. "It's just the truth."

"Well then maybe I need somewhere to plant my roots." He reached out with his foot and hooked her ankle. "Have a seat and enjoy the fire. She's gone to call Fancy Pants."

Fancy Pants? Simone said under her breath. Is that what they called Lincoln? Suddenly the tobacco flavor in her mouth tasted horrid.

Violet rested the dirty plate on the wide mantle, sat down on the ottoman and faced the fire. "I am tired," she sighed. "My work is never done."

Randolph moved behind her and began kneading her shoulders.

"I shouldn't let you do that," she said, "but it feels so good."

He rubbed the knobs on the back of her neck, slowly, softly, in tiny movements, as if her was tuning her in like a radio. "This," he said, gently squeezing either side of the base of her skull, "is called the jade pillow."

Simone couldn't hear what they were saying, not with their backs to her, so she slid along the living room wall and ducked into the library where she could get closer.

"That must have been hard for you at dinner," Randolph was saying. "So many mean words. I didn't know you had a sister. You can tell me about her if you want."

"Maybe another time," Violet said stretching her neck from side to side.

"You're such a hard worker, Violet. I really admire the way you manage the whole house. There's so much to do here and you're good at it all. My mother wasn't like that. She was only competent in one thing—music. She would play the organ all morning long, then lay on her bed the whole afternoon. She claimed she was delicate. *Une artiste*, she said. But I suspect she was just lazy. Like Simone."

Simone gawked silently. Lazy? She'd like to tell him a thing or two.

"Did she have a drinking problem, also?" Violet asked. Randolph nodded.

What? That was outrageous. They were accusing her of being a drunk. How absurd.

"And your father," Violet said to Randolph. "Did he love your mother? I think that's the real problem here. Simone is so unloved."

How dare she? thought Simone. Cavorting with Randolph, slandering her. What does she know about me? Simone crept from the library into the sunroom, though of course there was no sun. Nor moon. Not even stars. Only the black, cold night and a polar landscape of ice and snow.

She sank down on her knees on the hard tile floor. She hated Ann Arbor. She hated every time her mother-in-law looked her up and down with her disapproving eye. She hated her father-in-law and the blank slate behind his eyes. He never even saw her—or anyone else—it seemed. He resided in the house but he didn't live here. She hated Lincoln, too, and his possessive touch when he paraded her on his arm in public, like his latest toy. Even more she hated his private touch, the way he maneuvered her body for his own pleasure, forcing himself into her like she was his private garden to plant and till according to his desires. She was glad he was gone for a few days. Maybe the tender spot inside her would have a chance to heal.

And now she hated the awful things Randolph and Violet were saying about her. But what hurt even more was to see the gentle way Randolph touched Violet's shoulders and comforted her with kind words.

A series of bright arpeggio notes rang out from the piano. Two voices started singing a Negro spiritual, "Go Down Moses." Simone picked herself up off the sunroom floor and blew her nose into the hem of her terry cloth robe. Her skin had become cold; she was numb inside. She felt more a stranger in the house than the servants who got paid. Or was it money that kept her here, too? She had known after only a few weeks—sixteen weeks, to be exact, the night she lost the first baby—that her marriage was a mistake. But what could she do? She had no talent or skills to support herself. And she could never go home. Her mother made it clear when she got engaged that Simone was choosing to run away. "Just like when you were a little girl. You've never been satisfied in your own backyard." Besides, her family thought the Blankwell's were the cream of the crop. How could she go home and say she didn't feel loved?

She crept silently through the front of the living room. The two at the piano were intent on harmony: *"Thus spoke the Lord," bold Moses said, "If not, I'll smite your first born dead."* If only she had a first born. But God had smote all her babies before they had a chance to live. She climbed the stairs wearily and went to bed.

Chapter 20

"SHE MUST HAVE GONE TO BED," Violet said to Randolph as she brought him an armful of clean sheets from the upstairs linen closet. "I'm sure she'll understand you had to sleep in the house. And I'm sure she would agree that it's best for you to sleep down here in Ambra's room. She wouldn't want to come across you upstairs—or on a sofa—in the middle of the night." Or vice-versa, she thought.

He fiddled with the radio in the kitchen while she made up the bed. He had lost reception for *"The Rite of Spring."* But no worries, he smiled to himself. This storm was turning out even better than he dreamed. "They say all main roads are closed," he called out to Violet. "Over seven inches of snow, but the drifts are three feet high. Freezing rain cemented the whole thing together. Even the university is closed tomorrow. They're telling everybody to stay home."

"You can use the striped towels in the bathroom. The green ones are mine." She locked the back door out of habit and turned off the overhead light.

"There's a lock on my door, too, just in case you were wondering." She didn't tell him it was useless since there wasn't a key. "Let's hope tomorrow is a better day." She had to keep herself from repeating her mother's goodnight blessing: *May the sun of righteousness rise with healing in its wings.* But that's what she wanted, she wanted healing for herself, for Simone, even for Randolph, though she wasn't quite sure what his ailment might be.

"I'm sure tomorrow will be *extraordinaire.*" He blew her a kiss and went into the bedroom adjacent to hers.

Chapter 21

VIOLET AWOKE AT QUARTER TO SIX just like she did every morning. The sun wouldn't be up for an hour, but even without light she could sense a stillness outdoors. The wind had stopped howling. She leaned from her bed and peeked out the eastern window over the bits of colored glass, smooth as silk, which she had lined up on her narrow windowsill. It was such a luxury to have her own room, her own bed. At home in Missouri she shared a bed with Rosie, while her three brothers slept together in another bed across the room. Mama slept on a cot in the kitchen.

Now the house was quiet. Instead of the normal early morning sound of Ambra's heavy breathing, she heard a low drone through the knotty pine wall separating her from Randolph's sleeping body. The rooms in this back part of the house by the kitchen were built differently from the rest of the house. They had bead and batten walls instead of thick plaster. She loved it; it felt like home.

From the time she was a tiny girl her mother had taught

her to spend the first few minutes of the day sitting quietly in bed—while Rosie was still asleep—reading the Bible and turning her thoughts to God. "Like gathering manna," her Mama said, "breakfast for the soul. Man doesn't live by bread alone but by every word proceeding from the mouth of the Father." Here at the Blankwell's Violet kept her Bible hidden in the back of her closet. She'd been afraid to leave it in Missouri; that would have broken Mama's heart. But she hadn't opened its pages to read it since she'd arrived in Michigan. She didn't need to. Its words circled through her head like sparrows over the fields back home.

But she still liked the habit of starting her day with a few minutes of reading. Not long after she moved into the old farmhouse, she asked Mrs. Blankwell if she might borrow a book from the library every once in awhile.

"Of course, Violet, how wonderful," Mrs. B had said. "Nothing builds character more than fine literature. You know what Mark Twain said, don't you?"

Violet wasn't quite sure. She knew he was a famous writer. She was from Missouri after all.

"He said the man who doesn't read good books has no advantage over the man who can't read at all. So read away, but be sure to insert one of those index cards from the box on the desk to mark the book's place on the shelf in case someone in the family needs to use it."

Every few weeks Violet went into the library when no one else was home and let her eyes roam hungrily over the leather and clothbound feast. There were tiny old books whose pages had gold edging and great thick heavy books with paper jackets and enough pages for a whole year. Big books lay on their sides, with color plates protected by stiff frosty paper. A polished wooden box with a diagonal lid sat on the floor in one corner. It housed five giant books with summaries and illustrations of all the famous operas. The room even had a fancy step stool for reaching the highest shelves where some of the books were written in other languages. One whole shelf held a collection of yearbooks from the boarding schools and colleges where Mr. and Mrs. B and Lincoln had gone.

The library housed more than books. One wall had a built-in glass-front case harboring odd silver goblets and bowls inside. Loving cups, Mrs. B called them. They had engraving on the sides and almost all of them said Lincoln Ernest Blankwell and the dates were old, as far back as '05. Mr. B must have been a fine athlete—golf, tennis, football, shot put, and crew. There was even one for a state spelling contest won by Mrs. B in 1910.

Next to the loving cups hung some framed photographs. She could recognize Mr. B in his football uniform kneeling in the front row of his team. Another showed him sitting on a split rail fence dressed in a letter sweater, but it was a phony picture—the fence was set up indoors in front of a big painting of a meadow. She liked looking at these photos and trying to see old Mr. Blankwell in that young man's face. Lincoln took after his mother, with a long pointed nose and grey eyes the color of doves. It was a soft, tender color—one you would expect to find in a kind face. But Violet noticed that those liquid eyes could change to stone in less than a blink. Mr. B's face was rounder and gentler with a nose that had grown wide and fat since his college years.

But there was another photo, a more recent one of a

jazz ensemble with Lincoln when he was in college—it said so on the back. He was holding a clarinet and standing next to a man, the singer, who was dressed like a woman. Violet never would have recognized Lincoln because his face and neck and hands, like all the men in the group, was painted black. She wanted to take the photo out of its frame, shred it to bits, and throw it in the fire. What was wrong with these people? They hijacked Negro music, then made fun of the people who created it.

She pulled the bedspread up around her shoulders and turned on the reading lamp next to her bed. For the last two weeks she had been making her way through the poems of Robert Frost. It had been hard going at first— his words sounded stiff and thin. But listening over and over to the Psalms and Prophets had developed her taste for poetry and she recognized in Frost a man who loved the outdoors like she did. He had a poem for every kind of weather, for all sorts of trees and birds, for stars and flowers. He wrote about things she knew and described feelings she had never heard put to words. She could tell he was a sad man who was not quite sure that all would be well in the end. She wasn't sure either, though Mama said the Bible told the end of the story, and it was glorious for all who believed.

She made a tent with her knees and fluffed her pillow behind her back. Her bookmark—a pressed oak leaf—was set next to a poem she had read earlier in the week, "Storm Fear." Almost a prophecy of yesterday. She read through it again. The last lines haunted her, *"And my heart owns a doubt / Whether 'tis in us to arise with day / And save our- selves unaided."* She knew what her mother would say. Of course we can't save ourselves unaided. We all need a savior. But Violet wasn't so sure. Hadn't she been doing well on her own, working hard, sending half her money back home for Mama and Rosie and the boys? She'd learned how to slide through the rich man's world like an unseen spirit, and she was good at keeping her mouth shut—until last night. It had finally been too much for her. And Randolph divining the future through bird carcasses—that was evil, she was sure of it. They might as well have invited Satan and his minions to dinner. Maybe they had. Maybe that's what got into them all, made Randolph so lewd and Simone so foul-mouthed and uppity. Maybe that's why she had lost control and lashed out with hatred. For it was true, she had felt burning white hatred when that girl who had everything in the world said despicable things about Rosie.

Violet knew she'd better get up, with or without a savior. She had work to do. Work was her savior. She got out of bed and tucked her sheets and covers neatly under the quilt. Up against her pillow she propped the small pine-needle-stuffed pillow her mother had made for her out of remnants of an old dress. They didn't have family photographs so her mother embroidered their likenesses on the calico fabric: Mama standing in her apron on the front step of their small house with the dogs lying in the dirt at her side, her brothers perched in the branches of the willow tree. She was leaning back in the tire swing, that same swing where she had found and lost Earl Brown. And Rosie—her precious twin Rosie—was sitting in her wheelbarrow in front of the house with a big smile on her face.

Rosie. There was an ache in her heart for Rosie. The bed was so empty some nights without her sister's elbow knobbing into her back. And days were dreary and long without the sweetness of Rosie's cheerful face. What good were fancy clothes and a big house and a garage full of cars when there was no love? Her family was pure gold compared to the bitter brass of the Blankwells. She knew what brass was like. You could rub and polish door knockers and andirons every week to make them look good for awhile, but soon they turned cloudy and dark. Real gold always shown bright and true.

She tried not to think about Simone's awful words from the night before. Simone had accepted her apology and everything was fine. But Simone's mean spirit kept pricking her heart. It wasn't just the words; it was the haughty look on her face when she said them. It was as if a wicked beast slept inside Simone and woke up from time to time and possessed her. As the memories circled in Violet's head she felt the pain over and over. That's resentment, her mother would say, don't let "re-sentimenting" dig a hole of bitterness in your heart. Ask Jesus to forgive you.

But wasn't it Simone who needed forgiveness, not her? How did Simone even know about Rosie? Would Mrs. B have told her? She seemed above that sort of talk, especially with her daughter-in-law. Those two women were as unfriendly as blue jays, jabbing and flapping and scolding each other behind their backs.

Violet went to her closet. Only one clean uniform left. Did she really have to wear it today? She would much prefer her corduroys and wooly cardigan. Would Simone even care? The boundaries had already been blurred by the three of them eating together in the kitchen. Besides, it was Thursday, her regular afternoon off, though nothing seemed regular this week. She'd take a risk and wear her own clothes; if Simone didn't like it, then she'd change to her uniform later. But just in case, as a precaution, she'd fix French pancakes and bacon for breakfast, Simone's favorite.

She dressed and quickly brushed her hair, weaving it into two thick braids. As she headed to the bathroom she began to hum, *"When Israel was in Egypt land, oppressed so hard they could not stand,"* the song she and Randolph had sung together at the piano the night before.

To split a house in two, the house mover looks for places where two walls are flush with each other, so he can cut through the middle and still have both sides standing. Otherwise he has to build new walls to support the ceiling and the rooms above.

Chapter 22

WATER WAS RUNNING. Randolph woke with a start. Where was he? Oh yes, the storm. He had slept in Ambra's room. The bathroom sink on the other side of the wall made a loud gurgling sound as it sucked water down the drain. Then he heard a voice singing like an angel. Violet was up and ready for a new day. He sprang from bed, still wearing his underwear and socks from yesterday. He detested dirty clothes but he'd have to wait until later to get fresh things from his room. If it meant more time in the big house with the girls, he'd put up with a little odor and muss. He'd done it for two years in France; he could do it for two days here.

The one small window in Ambra's room faced north. The snow drifts were so high he had to stand on his toes to see over them into the yard where the storm had created a surrealistic landscape with sweeping wind-carved shapes held in place by frozen rain. He put on his glasses to get a sharper view. This was how he imagined the Arctic must look. The sun, just coming up, cast an eerie pink glow over the snowy architecture. Unless the radio announcer was mistaken and a heat wave hit, he had an excuse for another housebound day.

He pulled on his pants and peeked out the door. Violet was in the kitchen, her back toward him, filling the tea-kettle at the sink. The morning sun lit up her hair like a bronze fire. But something was odd—she wasn't wearing her regimental blue uniform. His eyes lingered on the long line of her legs beneath her slacks. Her sweater hugged the curve of her hips. As he ducked into the bathroom he remembered he didn't have his razor. Would Lincoln or the old man have an extra lying around? Or maybe he'd let his whiskers grow. He'd been wondering how he'd look with a beard. He'd ask the girls what they thought. The smell of bacon made him hurry through his washing. He scrubbed his knuckles and fingernails. No need to chop wood today; after breakfast he could go straight to his practicing—on the *grand* piano. What more could he ask for?

He finished dressing and went to the kitchen.

"Good morning," he said peering over Violet's shoulder. "What have we here? Crêpes Suzette? Starting the day with dessert, are we? Not an encore of flying strawberry short cake I hope."

Violet ignored him. "You could help by setting the table. Just two places. I imagine she will want a tray in her room."

"Too bad I can't cut her highness a perfect rose." He

saw Violet stiffen. Rose was her sister. He remembered too late. "Sorry," he mumbled. "Where can I find a clean table-cloth? I'd need a schematic drawing to keep track of all the possessions in this house."

"Bottom drawer on the left side of the pantry, below the glasses. Bring the one with the blue and white checks."

He went into the pantry and stood between the two walls lined with cupboards and drawers. How could one family use all these things? Silver pitchers that had to be polished, great serving trays with painted turkeys and rabbits, red and green dishes for Christmas, ones with yellow flowers for spring, and a whole set of orange plates and bowls shaped like pumpkins.

As he bent to open the tablecloth drawer, he kicked something. Simone's high-heeled, pink satin slippers scattered across the floor. He picked them up and fingered their smooth surface, cradling one in each palm. They were barely as long as his hand.

"What are you doing out there?" Violet called. "No chance of pilfering. Mrs. B has me count every piece of silver the first of each month."

He found the tablecloth and closed the drawer. "Coming," he said and tucked the slippers in his pockets. "Is this the one you want?"

She nodded. "Spread it out and have a seat. Your pancakes are ready."

"Just let me, umm." He tried to think of an excuse to go back to Ambra's room and deposit the shoes.

"Randolph?" Violet turned and looked at him.

"Great," he said sitting down with a grunt as the high heels pressed into his thighs.

"I don't know what to think of you this morning, Randolph. You look like a grizzly bear and you sound like one too." She slid a plate of rolled up pancakes in front of him.

"I don't know what to think of you either—in your civvies. Planning on taking the day off?" He cut a pancake in two with his fork and popped it in his mouth.

"Wouldn't I love to, but who would cook and wash and clean?"

"We could eat cold chicken and go dirty." He took another bite of breakfast. "And eat dessert all day."

"Besides, can we even get outside? I wouldn't consider a day stuck in this house to be a day off."

"I'll see what I can do about liberating you a little later," he said.

She cocked her chin toward the ceiling to listen. "The tub's emptying upstairs." She settled a plate of pancakes on a wicker tray and covered them with a warming lid. "I'm going to try and start this day on the right foot," she said. "You behave."

As soon as Violet was halfway up the back stairs, he tiptoed to Ambra's room and hid the slippers under the bed.

Chapter 23

SIMONE AWOKE WITH A THROBBING HEADACHE. Bright sunlight, intensified by the snow, streamed through the eastern window. She'd forgotten to pull the drapes the night before. She covered her eyes with her forearm and burrowed deeper under the covers. She wasn't ready for another day. Her mind fumbled for the fraying edges of a dream. She wanted to grab hold of those phantom thoughts, like the tail strings of a kite driven by the wind of her subconscious, and let them pull her over today, beyond tomorrow, out to an ocean of forgetfulness.

It was almost working. She lay back down on the porch swing at the house on Swan Street, her legs bent, her skirt wrapped close around her knees. The viburnum was in bloom and she was twirling a pinky-white fragrant cluster under her nose while Toby strummed his guitar. Every so often she trailed a foot and pushed off from the floor. The chains holding the swing creaked in time to Toby's music. Only in her dream the sound was not just aural, it had color: dark blue and shaped like a cat, a smoky blue cat with long soft fur. Toby was petting the cat and the cat was singing. The cat's whiskers became the strings of the guitar. Then the cat was howling. Toby was strumming its belly. He was strumming her belly. He was howling. She reached down to stop his hand; his fingers were strings, bloody strings. He had no fingers. She woke in a sweat. Her fingers dripped with blood.

She shrieked and threw off her covers. There it was, another pool of blood. Not a pool exactly, more like a round red spot the size of a dinner plate. She stuffed her nightgown between her legs and limped to the bathroom. Why wasn't Ambra here when she needed her? From the toilet she leaned to the tub and turned on the cold water. Cold water takes out blood; hot water sets the stain. That's what her mother said. She lifted the gown over her head and gobbed it under the faucet. At least it wasn't one of her good silk gowns from her trousseau, just a cotton eyelet one left over from before she was married. The water bloomed pink in the white porcelain tub.

Her terrycloth robe lay crumpled on the floor where she'd left it last night. She pulled it around her shaking body and turned on the hot water in the sink, lathering up her washcloth for a sponge bath. Her insides were rebelling against her, insisting to come out. But that only happened at night while she was asleep, when her defenses were down; that's what she told herself. That was the lie she believed. When she got dressed each morning she pretended the clean fresh under things and the carefully chosen outfits that fit so well on her slim, boyish body were a kind of armor that camouflaged her from the world. She would look at her neat reflection in the mirror and feel under control. She couldn't see the invisible forces that animated her body and drove her every thought and word.

She rinsed out the wash cloth and hung it on the towel bar. What had she been dreaming about when she woke up? There was music and a cat and—oh no—Toby MacIntire. Toby, the fastest runner on the block. The boy who teased that her legs were too skinny. The boy who wanted to play with those same skinny legs a few years later. Toby who made the most beautiful music with his guitar, sad Irish songs he'd learned from his father. Toby with straight black bangs hiding his bluebird eyes, till he flung them away with a toss of his head that always said yes. Yes said his chin, yes smiled his eyes, yes sang his fingers as they danced over the hole in his guitar, as they danced over her summer skin.

She bit hard into the fat side of her first finger between the two big knuckles to keep from crying. Toby had danced his way into another hole, a foxhole. A German rocket blew away his hand and all the music in him, all the laughter; even the blue of his eyes had drained out and disappeared into foreign soil. When the army sent him home, he sat on his front porch on the other side of Swan Street, across from her house, and wouldn't even smile when she turned cartwheels on the lawn outside his house. He wouldn't talk to her or look at her face; he didn't want to touch her anymore. It was worse for her than having him away at war. She would almost feel better if he had died in battle; then at least all her memories would be happy ones. Now she just felt like a failure, as if part of her were dead too. The way he ignored her made her feel ugly and unattractive.

So when she met the handsome Lincoln Blankwell,

Jr. while visiting her brother in Bethesda—they were in the Navy, stateside, together—she welcomed the attention from a wealthy, well-bred, Ivy League man who was all in one piece. He was older and he talked like he knew where he was going and wanted to take her along. She aligned her compass with his North and never looked back. Until one morning, a week before the wedding, a tiger kitten appeared in a box on her porch with a red bow around its neck. She knew where it came from. She refused to cry. She hardened her heart and made her mother take it to the pound. It was too late. That dream was gone forever.

She brought her hand to her mouth again. Two rows of dark blue teeth marks indented her flesh. Where was Lincoln today when she needed him? Why hadn't he called? Was it just the storm or had he found another way to amuse himself? His old flame, Ginny Needhouse, lived near Chicago. Maybe he was—she bit down hard again. Pain shot through her finger like electricity. She was working herself into a fit. That's what Lincoln would call it. She was imagining the worst, he'd say, being over dramatic. Histrionic. Another one of his fancy words.

She went into the bedroom and opened her old friend Yeats. As a rule she tried not to drink before breakfast, but this day was already looking bad. The vodka burned on the way down her throat. Her body started to relax. She took a deep breath, another swig. Everything would be okay. It had to have been the storm that kept him from calling. He adored her; he always said so. So she'd better calm down. She had to take charge.

She cleaned herself up, got dressed in her old blue jeans and a soft turtleneck. The only thing she could do with her hair—it was an absolute fright after drying in the towel last night—was to braid it into pigtails. So what if she looked twelve years old? No one would see her today. From the view out her window, all the world had stopped. High drifts of snow covered the yard, and the sun gleamed off the surface as if a coating of glass had been laid down on top of everything. Not one vehicle passed on the road. She was marooned.

She lit a cigarette, then picked a fleck of tobacco off her tongue. She'd make the best of it. She'd immerse herself in art. She'd keep her distance from the help. No more nasty scenes like last night. What foolishness. She could handle things better than that. She would be who she really was: Mrs. Lincoln Blankwell Junior.

Before going downstairs for breakfast, she went into the bathroom and pulled the plug from the tub, letting the water drain. She hid the bloody mess of sheets and nightgown behind the shower curtain. Out of sight, out of mind.

Chapter 24

FOR MRS. BLANKWELL SENIOR, the old farmhouse was her *grand oeuvre*, a work of art. In the months before her wedding back in 1915, she had scoured the countryside around Ann Arbor for the optimal location from which to present herself—and her soon-to-be-successful husband—to society. She was no young bride like Simone. She'd finished college and done the Grand Tour: Europe, of course, including Morrocco. The Middle East complete with a camel trek to the pyramids and then a stop in Istanbul. Then she'd crossed North America by train to board a steamer to the Orient, and on her way back from China been shipwrecked off the coast of Japan. She knew a thing or two. She presumed she would one day have children. But whether or not that came to pass, she needed rooms for entertaining, rooms for overnight guests, and rooms for the help—not to mention a grand fireplace or two, a study, a library, and an ample butler's pantry to house the ample wedding gifts that had already begun to arrive.

The house itself had to be well built. No sagging

porches or uneven floors, heaven forbid. She insisted on classical lines but was willing to give an inch or two in favor of charm. Presentation was of utmost importance. No ostentatious exhibitionist gloating over itself right in public view. No, her perfect dwelling would be at the end of a long winding drive, appearing much smaller than actuality, giving the favored guest the intimate perception that he alone was privy to its marvelous, mysterious expanse.

So property became nearly as important as structure. A copse, a glade, a pond, a creek; a cutting garden, a sunning garden, an herbaceous border; a stand of poplar, a thicket of sumac; a wide rolling lawn, a private enclosed walk—these were her requirements, along with the third leg of her platform after presentation and property: proximity.

It wouldn't do to live in Ann Arbor proper. Who wanted to be labeled a city-dweller, or pay those taxes? But it was equally foolish to live way out in nowhere. Who would visit? What about parties? So she procured the most current plat of Washtenaw County, employed her protractor and compass left over from college geometry, and zeroed in on the possibilities. Once the prime location was determined and existing properties surveyed, she kept a hawkish eye on the obituary page. Before long Providence smiled: old Mr. McMaster who had inherited the original homestead from his father fell prey to influenza. Harriet Haggersmith, the soon-to-be Mrs. Blankwell, swooped in.

That's not to say work didn't have to be done. Fields were plowed under and seeded with something more dignified than corn, blackberry brambles were replaced with lilacs, the pear orchard pruned, and peonies were planted along the drive. The old barn was transformed into a handsome garage with an upstairs apartment. Her father in Lansing drove a brand new Cadillac and she was forward looking enough to know that the time was soon approaching when garage space would be at a premium. She had a breezeway built between the garage and the house and a wide circular bench constructed around the old oak in the middle of the back lawn, the centerpiece of her flower borders and the site of many anticipated social events.

But the jewel in the crown, the plum in the pudding, the feather in Mrs. Blankwell's hat, was the miniature Chinese scholar's garden she designed from memory from her visit to Suzhou, Jiangsu Province, China.

Chapter 25

VIOLET WAS JUST ABOUT TO KNOCK on the bedroom door when Simone opened it from inside. "Oh!" they said at the same time, looking into each other's faces, at their girlish hairstyles, and their casual clothes.

"I've brought you breakfast in bed," Violet said. "But I see you're already up."

"I am," Simone said.

"So...."

"So why don't I come down and eat in the kitchen? It must be cheerful in there at this time of day," Simone said, completely ignoring her earlier resolve to stay away from the help.

"Or the sunroom," Violet suggested. "Mrs. Blankwell Sr. often takes her morning coffee there." Violet dreaded the three of them together in the kitchen again. Besides, she wasn't sure how Simone would react when she found out Randolph had slept in the house last night.

Violet stepped back from the door to let Simone pass and followed her down the front stairs, waiting to see which way she would turn. How different the house felt this morning, with the sun angling in through the south windows, resting softly on the Oriental rug in front of the fireplace. Simone stepped from the bottom of the stairs into the living room, then turned left and headed for the library and the sunroom beyond. Violet gave a silent sigh of relief.

"This is a good idea, Violet. I'll sit in here and enjoy the peace and quiet."

Violet set the tray down on the glass-topped table and removed the warming cover from Simone's plate. "I hope they're still warm," she said. "Would you like a pot of tea?"

"French pancakes? Oh my." She poked a crêpe with her fingertip. "It's fine. And I'd love some good strong tea." The mess she had left upstairs disappeared from her mind like a small puff of cloud on a bright summer day. Simone was a chameleon: she adapted her personality to the room she was in. Her surroundings, not the feelings inside her, informed her emotions.

"I'll be back as soon as the water boils."

Simone looked around her. It hardly seemed like the same room she'd been crying in last night. This morning it was flooded with light bouncing off the snowy whiteness outdoors. The sunroom was her mother-in-law's winter kingdom. In the back, out of reach from direct sun, an elaborate bent wire "tree" held pots of furry-leafed gloxinia and violets. They were all in bloom: white, pink, violet, deep purple. Along the wall that separated the sunroom from the Chinese garden outside were troughs full of forced spring bulbs. Mrs. Blankwell kept a steady supply ready in the root cellar and brought them up when they were about to open. Tiny paperwhites and sturdy hyacinths gave off a glorious sweet smell. Simone had to admit Lincoln's mother was a wizard with flowers. Everyone she met in Ann Arbor told her she would simply die when she saw the outdoor gardens in spring.

Violet returned with a second tray weighed down with the big teapot in its quilted cozy, a pitcher of cream, and a bowl of sugar. Both the Mrs. Blankwells liked their tea the English way. "Will that be all, Ma'am?" It didn't seem right to Violet to call her Simone today.

"Yes," Simone said. "And Violet, I'd like to be alone," she added. "In fact, I'll be in the study later and don't want to be disturbed."

"But do you mind?" Violet asked.

"Mind what?"

"My clothes, Ma'am. Is it all right if I don't wear my uniform today?"

Simone hesitated. How was she supposed to decide?

"Don't worry, I won't be taking the afternoon off like I usually do on Thursdays. But I thought maybe…."

Simone interrupted: "That things could be a bit less formal today since everyone's gone and we've had the storm and all?"

"I'll fix the meals and do the laundry—and anything else you want me to do," Violet said.

"That's fine, Violet. Dress how you want and have an easy day. You don't need to bother with my rooms until tomorrow," forgetting the mess she left upstairs in the tub.

"Thank you, Ma'am." She left the room.

Simone curled her legs under her on the love seat and let her mind go blank as her eyes wandered over the shapes and colors of the flowers. Something about color made her ache. Not in a painful way, at least not usually. It was as if she were a tuning fork and different colors struck deep vibrations within her. A sudden break in the clouds, a swath of blue after days of grey blindness felt like life itself. That blue, the promise of space, of expanse, pierced her with a longing for something more real than the world around her. Or sunshine gold, the color of alchemy, danced in her with a brilliant song that flew out to her fingertips and pressed hard against her chest, like a fiery bird caught in a cage.

Chapter 26

WHEN VIOLET GOT BACK TO THE KITCHEN, Randolph was washing his dishes. "Aren't you the helpful one," she said going to the stove to fix her own breakfast. When Ambra was there the two of them ate before anyone else was up, but this morning Violet had taken more time than usual with her reading.

"I like putting my hands in water," he said. "It softens the calluses I get from the woodpile." He wiped his hands on a dishtowel. "Why don't you let me cook pancakes for you?"

"Don't be silly. You can't cook. Especially not French pancakes. They're very particular."

He swatted her with the towel. "Step back my dear and be amazed. I hail from the country of cuisine."

She giggled in spite of herself. "All right. I'll put up my feet and take my ease while you serve me." She fished an old copy of *Life* magazine out of the paper bin. "By the way," she said. "*She* says she'll be busy in the study all morning and doesn't want to be disturbed until lunch."

"Oh, she doesn't, does she? Don't worry, I won't bother

her. When I'm finished with this I'm going to do my practicing at the *grand* piano. I could get used to living here."

"Dream on," Violet said. "An opportunity like this only comes once in a blue moon."

"And when will the next one of those be?" Randolph turned over the thin pancake he was cooking and went to look at the kitchen calendar that showed the major phases of the moon. He flipped through the months until he came to August. "Ah ha. This must be a lucky year—two full moons in August. And no black moons at all."

"Black moon? What's that?"

"Let me roll this crêpe for you—a little butter and powdered sugar—and I'll tell you about black moons." He set her plate before her and sat down. "In New Orleans, my home, everything is jumbled together like a good jambalaya."

"Like what?" Violet looked up from her breakfast.

"Jambalaya," he said again. "A kind of stew with whatever you want—ham and shrimp and sausage and chicken and all sorts of vegetables and lots of spices." He pointed to her empty plate. "I see my cooking wasn't too terrible."

"I have to admit they're delicious." She'd never been waited on like this, not even at home when she'd been sick for three weeks with scarlet fever. The day was beginning to feel as bright as the snow outside. The pancakes had been more like dessert than breakfast and she felt almost giddy with hope that the disaster of last night was forgotten and today they could have fun.

"New Orleans is half water and half land," Randolph continued. "Most of the land we do have is below sea level. The people are half Negro, half White. The Creoles are half French, half Spanish. The religion is all mixed up, too with carnival season starting on Twelfth Night and going to Mardi Gras—Pancake Day."

"I've heard of Mardi Gras but I thought it was a wild party, not part of religion."

"That's the jumble. Mumbo jumbo. Voodoo. Baron Samedi and Mother Mary rolled into one."

As she took her plate to the sink a cold feeling crept up her spine again. Why did he keep mentioning religion, mixing Christian talk with black magic?

"And a black moon," he went on, "is a second new moon in one month—two nights of utter darkness."

The shiver spread across her neck.

"Those acquainted with such sport say that magic under a black moon has twice as much power."

"You're talking about witches, aren't you? Witches and demons—and Satan." She shouldn't listen to him. He was a dangerous man. "I don't believe in that stuff," she said, as much to herself as to him. She went to the refrigerator and took out the bowl of cold chicken. She decided right then what she'd make for lunch—chicken salad, with the bones removed and thrown in the trash. She wasn't going to take any chances.

"It's not what you think, Violet. Louisiana magic comes from Africa. It has nothing to do with the devil. The witches in the northeast who came over from England with the rich white folk, they're the ones who brought black magic to this country."

"It's all bad if you ask me. Nothing good can come from taking power into your own hands."

He got up from the table. "Speaking of hands I'm going

to give mine some exercise. Then I'll see what I can do about getting one of the doors open so we can go outside."

That would be a relief, she thought. She needed to get out of the house and away from Randolph and Simone, if only for an hour or two. People talked about needing a breath of fresh air; she needed to breathe in God's spirit, the holiness of creation. She looked longingly out the window and saw two squirrels huddled together on the back of the wooden seat that had been built around the large oak in the back yard. She watched them as she mixed the chopped chicken pieces with onion and celery and sprinkled the salad with paprika. One squirrel had its tail over its back like a fur coat; the other curled its tail down and underneath itself. The two were rubbing noses. When a third squirrel ran down from a higher branch, the curled-tail squirrel left its friend and chased the other away. When it returned, it nuzzled its friend, then mounted her back. They poked their noses into each other's undersides and sat up to preen each other's fur. Then the male—definitely the male—grabbed hold of the other and mounted again. The icy crust of snow broke loose and the two rolled off the narrow board and onto the seat and scampered away.

Chapter 27

A RUSH OF MUSIC startled Simone out of her reverie. Randolph. She finished the last of her tea and stood to stretch. Everything in her felt cramped. How long had she been sitting on the love seat with her legs folded beneath her, staring into the distance? Sometimes a whole hour or even a whole afternoon passed without her knowing where it had gone. Today she would be productive. Today she would take charge of her life. Today she was going to paint.

She left her breakfast dishes on the glass table and walked through the living room to the study. Randolph nodded in her direction. She gave him a little wave. What would her mother-in-law think if she saw him running his handyman fingers over her expensive ivory? It was a good thing there weren't any spies around the house taking snap shots of the last couple of days. Though it would be fun to have some pictures of the storm. Who would believe the fantastic shapes the wind had carved and whittled from ice and snow? Maybe she should try to paint what she saw out the window. But no, she was going to do what she had planned. That's what discipline meant. That's what mature people did.

She closed the door to the study until it made a secure click. She had told Violet she wanted to be alone and that was that. Randolph would be busy with his practice for two hours or more; Violet would be doing whatever it was she did. And she would draw and paint.

Her paints and paper were still on the sofa where she'd left them yesterday afternoon, along with her flask of water. It seemed like a week since she had climbed the drive with wet feet. She'd better retrieve her loafers from the radiator before they turned to paper. And where were her pink high heels, the ones she'd worn to dinner last night? She distinctly remembered running up the back stairs barefoot—the rough rubber treads had hurt her feet.

She left the room and went to the front hall and picked up her loafers. They were nice and toasty. Then she went around the stairway, avoiding the piano, through the dining room and pantry and into the kitchen. Violet was sweeping the floor.

"Did you find my pink satin shoes, the ones I was wearing last night?" She took a pitcher from the drain board and filled it with water for her paints.

"No Ma'am, they're not in here. Did you look in the pantry?"

"I just came through there. You think I'm blind?"

"Of course not, I'm sorry. I'll go look for them."

"They're my Ferragamos, a Christmas present from Lincoln." And god-awful expensive, too, she thought to herself. Lincoln would kill her if she lost them. "I'll be in the study until lunch." She turned and left. A girl like Violet would have no idea who Salvatore Ferragamo was or how exquisite it felt to slip on a pair of his handmade shoes. It made Simone feel like a princess and she bet it made Lincoln feel like a king. He loved to dress her up in beautiful clothes.

Once in the study she opened her book of Van Gogh and flipped through the pages to find a print to copy. She stopped at three chalk and gouache paintings of the insane asylum where he had lived in Saint-Rémy. They showed complex interior scenes of a long corridor painted in ocherous yellows and dried-blood reds. She turned the page. She didn't want to think about the voices in his head. She had enough in her own.

There was a beautiful field of poppies but it was much too detailed for her to paint. She needed something more contained. Besides she could hardly imitate oil with water-color, not the thick, globby way Van Gogh painted. She found a watercolor he had done of stone steps in the gar-den of the asylum. That should work. She sat on the chair in front of the north window—the light was bright because of the snow—and began to sketch in the shapes.

She worked busily, trying to get the wall, the fence, and the trees in the right relationship to one another. Then she filled her water cup and started dabbing at the paper. That must be what Van Gogh had done, for there were no sweeping planes of color, no wet on wet painting; the whole picture was hundreds of jabbed-at brush strokes: blues and greens and browns on a yellow background. Her wrist was beginning to ache from so many little spots of color. Her picture was ugly—both her copy and the original. She threw her brush on the floor. What was the point? Van Gogh had been insane when he painted it. She ripped the page off her paper block and tore it in two.

Poor lonely Van Gogh. She ripped the paper again. So misunderstood. So unappreciated. She tore the pieces smaller and smaller. No one recognized his genius, no one cared about his art—until he was dead. Her lap was littered with flecks of paper. "My own private snow storm," she muttered as she flicked the colored fragments onto the floor and went to stare out the window. A cardinal couple was perched by the light post next to the front door: the male on the post, the female on the snow below. The male—opulent against the glaring background—flew down to his muted mate and passed her a morsel from his beak. Even the animal kingdom knew something of love and faithfulness.

She looked down and saw her book about Cézanne on the windowsill with a beautiful still life of poppies, orangey-red like the cardinal, on its cover. She would copy that. She set to work with her pencil, but sounds from the piano distracted her. Randolph was rushing up and down the scales, making a sound like waves crashing on a beach. Each surge of notes crested higher than the next, encroaching farther on to the shore. His power was frightening.

She turned back to the still life, trying hard to focus on details she hadn't noticed before, like the way one tulip leaf draped across another or how the apples and oranges disappeared off the edge of the table. Now Randolph was playing something slow and sneaky, as if his fingers barely touched the keys. He was creeping around, peering up over the top of high notes then disappearing into the recesses of dark notes. Was he wooing her? Could he sense she was listening? Was he telling her something, sending her a message? He shouldn't be in the house; his place was in the garage.

She opened her watercolor set and studied the way Cezanne used his colors: the vase was bright green like the poppy leaves, the flowers were deep red with pink and orange at their base, the background and table were a mottled turquoise blue. But what surprised her was that in the upper left-hand corner beyond the tallest tulip, Cézanne made the background dark purply-brown, just like the shadows under the table and behind the vase and the fruit. He used darkness to bring out brilliance. She became absorbed mixing her colors to match the ones in the original and didn't notice that the music stopped.

Once his calculations are clear and both sections of the house are reinforced with supporting walls, the house mover cuts through the exterior siding, down through the timbers, and up through the roof, making the separation parallel with the trusses and rafters.

Chapter 28

RANDOLPH SLID THE BENCH away from the piano, clasped his hands behind his back and stretched, lacing his fingers first one way then the other. He could have been playing for ten minutes or two hours. Music was his drug, perhaps like opium, he imagined. In France they had called opium the Yellow Whore, though he had never tried it. He preferred flesh and blood—or ebony and ivory. When he sat at the piano and his fingers started moving, stroking the keys, alone, together, in intricate patterns, hands together, hands apart, crossing over one another, fighting, racing, teasing, wooing, soothing, whispering, waiting, he dropped into another world like Alice into Wonderland. The mathematics of the universe spun out through him, the keyboard became a slide rule of emotions. Notes multiplied through chords and were factored out through sharps and flats. His mind skipped across the shoreless pond of sound like a smooth, flat stone.

He knew the importance of balance, of keeping every muscle and joint limber, making sure he had a full range of movement. He needed to be quick in his fingers—and on his toes. Ready to flee.

But not today. Despite what he'd told Violet, he wasn't going to open the cage just yet. Even if he could push a door against the heavy, banked snow, he wanted another day in the house, another evening to settle into the over-stuffed chair by the fire. He needed another night to prowl.

He got up from the piano bench and walked quietly through the living room. The door to the study was shut and sounds from upstairs told him Violet was vacuuming. He headed to the library. There was some research he wanted to do, to find out what sort of fellow Lincoln really was. He knew just where to look—in the old college yearbooks.

He moved the step stool over to the corner by the loving cups and reached up for a handful of *Banners*, 1935-1939, the heart of the Depression, though from the look of things life had gone on as usual in the Ivy Tower. He and Lincoln were nearly the same age only Randolph had worked his way through college in a butcher shop while the young Mr. "Bankwell," as Randolph liked to call him, kept busy raking in usury from the deposits in his savings account. Now Lincoln was out in the working world—though he was still living at home—while Randolph was getting a leg up on the GI Bill. Time would tell who made it to the top.

He started with the yearbook from Lincoln's senior

year. He was a fine looking fellow—physics club, tennis team, but what was this, *original member of the S.O.B.s*? He flipped through the pages until he spotted what he was looking for: *The Society of Orpheus and Bacchus, founded September 1938, meets every Tuesday night at Hyman's Temple Bar to sing specially arranged a cappella numbers.* Old Linc was a barroom singer? It was hard to imagine. He was stiff as a board around the house. A regular SOB. He chuckled.

He started to put the book back on the shelf, but it slipped from his fingers and landed on its back with the pages splayed open. The cover flexed and a folded piece of paper dislodged from a slit inside the front cover. The paper was stiff and dry as if it had been pressed between the pages for some time. Randolph glanced behind him at the door and listened. The vacuum purred upstairs. There was so sound from Simone. The girls were still about their business. He unfolded the paper. *To L* it said at the top. *You are my Song of Songs. May our nights never end.* Then there were some verses of poetry:

> *Kiss me with the kisses of your mouth—*
> *For your love is more delightful than wine.*
> *Take me away with you—let us hurry!*
> *Like an apple tree among the trees of the forest*
> *Is my lover among young men.*
> *I delight to sit in his shade and his fruit is sweet*
>   *to my taste.*
> *His left arm is under my head, and his right arm*
>   *embraces me.*

Randolph paused and pictured the scene in his mind.

Left arm under her head—he assumed this was written by a woman—and right arm embracing her. Ah yes. He read on.

> I slept but my heart was awake. Listen! My lover
>   is knocking:
> "Open to me, my sister, my darling, my dove, my
>   flawless one.
> My head is drenched with dew, my hair with the
>   dampness of the night."
> I have taken off my robe—must I put it on again?
> I have washed my feet—must I soil them again?
> My lover thrust his hand through the latch opening;
> My heart began to pound for him.
> I arose to open for my lover, and my hands dripped
>   with myrrh,
> My fingers with flowing myrrh, on the handles
>   of the lock.

Randolph grinned. This was great stuff—hands thrust through latch-openings, fingers dripping with myrrh. Who could have written it? It was hard to imagine old Linc inspiring such passion. He turned the page over.

> My lover has gone down to his garden, to the beds
>   of spices,
> To browse in the gardens and to gather lilies.
> I am my lover's and my lover is mine;
> He browses among the lilies.

Randolph liked to browse among lilies himself, down in those spicy beds. It reminded him of a certain spicy Creole girl he used to visit on hot nights back home.

Under the apple tree I roused you; there your mother
conceived you,
There she who was in labor gave you birth.
Place me like a seal over your heart, like a seal over
your arm;
For love is as strong as death, its jealousy unyielding
as the grave.
It burns like blazing fire, like a mighty flame.
Many waters cannot quench love; rivers cannot wash
it away.

At the bottom of the page was a crude colored-pencil drawing of an apple tree with red apples shaped like hearts. And below that, clear as day, was a tiny "V."

V? Could it be? This was a mystery—or was it? Whatever it was, it was a gold mine. Randolph refolded the letter and put it in his back pocket. He was ready for lunch with the ladies.

But first he needed to deposit his treasure in a safe place. He scooted through the living room and behind the stairway to avoid being seen by Violet upstairs. Her vacuuming had moved to the master bedroom. Then he took the dining room-pantry route to the back of the house, crouching low behind the loveseat as he passed the closed doorway to the study. Simone must still be in there dabbling at her watercolors. He loved this furtive dodging and hiding. It reminded him of crossing enemy lines in the war, sneaking through French villages, outsmarting the Germans. Because he spoke French he had been assigned to help the French Resistance. It had been great fun. And so was this. He loved intrigue.

He passed through the kitchen. The table was set for two and a tray was laid out for Simone. He went into Ambra's room and was about to tuck the letter under the mattress when he remembered the pink shoes. Just for fun he'd put them in Violet's closet and tuck the letter with them too.

He heard noise at the top of the stairs and hurried back to Ambra's room, hiding behind the door just in time to keep from being seen by Violet.

Chapter 29

Violet wrapped the cord around the brackets on the back of the vacuum cleaner and stored it in the upstairs cleaning closet. At least she didn't have to lug the heavy thing up and down stairs—Mrs. Blankwell had two vacuums. That was one of the things Violet admired in Mrs. B —she was practical and generous in the way she managed her affairs. Violet had learned a lot from observing Mrs. B over the past few months. If it wasn't for the emotional torrents which swept through the family as regularly as rain, she would almost enjoy working here. But she never knew when one relationship or another would overrun its banks and sweep away the bridges leaving her stranded.

She hung the feather duster on its hook, put away the Murphy's Oil Soap, and tossed the dirty rags in the corner at the top of the back stairs. She'd deal with those later. It was almost twelve; she'd better fix lunch. She could hear that Randolph was done with his practicing. Simone was probably done with her painting. But her work was never done. She could clean the house for ten hours a day and still find more to do. Did Randolph work up a sweat sitting at the piano bench? Did Simone get grit under her fingernails applying watercolors to paper? Why was her life so hard? Wasn't she allowed to have creative urges? Was she doomed to be a cleaning lady all her life—like her mother? Like her black-skinned mother, her daughter-of-a-slave mother? Was she predestined to live in cramped rooms and take the back stairs? What did Simone have—besides her milky skin—which entitled her to hold all the keys? Surely a soul had no color.

Resentment left her face as another thought seeped into her mind, like the warm rapeseed oil Mama used to drip over her corn-rowed head when she was a little girl. Her jaw softened with a flush of thankfulness. She was earning a fair wage. She had a room of her own and more food and clothes than she could ever use. She was strong and healthy and in her right mind—not haunted by demons day and night like poor Simone.

She glanced out the small hexagonal window that overlooked the kitchen roof. Snow had formed a series of peaks and valleys running parallel to the side of the house where she was standing. It was just about noon and the sun was nearly overhead. The absence of shadows played tricks on her eyes, making the snowy roof appear almost smooth. Pure light was like that, Violet thought. Like forgiveness. Pure light and pure love covered a multitude of sins. Last night she had been lucky. Simone had forgiven her.

And this morning Simone had told her to take it easy, to have a relaxing day. Well maybe she would. She'd obey the Missus and take time for herself. Even if she couldn't get outside and go for a walk, she'd retreat to her room, do something with the wild flowers she had pressed last summer and fall. Her Bible was bursting with them. At least that big book came in handy for something.

She skipped down the back stairs feeling free in her afternoon-off clothes. She was anxious for lunch to be over and her own time to begin.

Chapter 30

THERE WERE THREE INTERIOR WAYS into the kitchen. When the grandfather clock struck twelve Randolph emerged from the narrow passageway off Ambra's room just as Simone entered off the hall from the front of the house. When Violet pushed her way through the swinging pantry door a few seconds later, breadbasket in hand, she caught their two startled faces looking at her across the room. The happiness she had felt a moment before disappeared in the air like a soap bubble. She took a step back and lowered her eyes. Why did she feel like she was walking into a snare, that Randolph and Simone were weaving a scheme to trap her? Maybe the drama of the night before was part of a plan. She remembered the grip of Randolph's hands around her waist at the top of the stairs when he mistook her for Simone in the peacock kimono. Were the two of them up to something?

"Hello Violet," Randolph said, but she gave him one of her cold stares. He adjusted his target to Simone. "Hello Mrs. Blankwell. We meet again." He couldn't help grinning;

with her hair done up in braids, she looked like a little girl. How long would it take him to get them undone? That would be a good goal for this afternoon.

"Hello Randolph," Simone said to him, then noticed the table. "Set only for two again?" she said. "Is this some sort of conspiracy?" She laughed. "Are you trying to banish me, Violet?"

"Oh no, Ma'am," Violet flushed, while Randolph crossed the room and took hold of Simone's elbow.

"We'd be more than delighted to have you join us *again*," he said with an extra beat on the last word. He was thrilled with the way the pieces were falling into place. He pulled out the chair where Simone had sat the night before.

"Thank you," she said. "I know this is all a bit unusual, with the Blankwells gone and Lincoln away. And I miss Ambra. She's such a dear."

"I readied you a tray in case…"

"Forget it," Simone said with a snap.

"Forgive and forget, that's what I always say," said Randolph, hoping neither woman would forget the night before. He felt most alive in a room full of tension. It gave him an extra zing, like moving fast, skating on top of frozen ice, banking sharp blades first on one side, then the other, zigzagging his way ahead.

Violet put a third place setting at the table and set out the basket of bread. She took the dish of chicken salad from the refrigerator and a plate of lettuce with sliced tomatoes. There was a jar of canned peaches and some gingersnaps for dessert. Mrs. B said no meal was complete without a taste of fruit.

"Forgiveness, now that's a big subject," Simone said. "Am I right in remembering your father's a minister?"

"Was," Randolph said. "He's dead. But forgiveness wasn't a big part of his theology."

"No?" asked Simone.

"He didn't need it since he didn't believe in sin."

Violet sat down and passed the bread to Simone. She hoped neither of them would expect her to say grace today.

"Oh, I'm so sorry," Simone said. "I didn't know."

"That he's dead or that he didn't believe in sin?" Randolph liked to fluster her.

She cut her sandwich in half. "That's not funny. I was born Catholic. Death and sin are serious subjects."

The wages of sin is death, thought Violet as she spread chicken salad over her bread. *But the gift of God is eternal life.* That's where she'd get her reward according to her mother—the hereafter. *So give thanks always and learn to be content in any circumstance.* These unsolicited memory verses were getting to be a nuisance. Her thoughts had made her miss part of the conversation. Now Simone was spouting off one of her half-baked opinions.

"I think," Simone said, "it's a question of balance. If you do enough good things—more good than bad—then you'll go to heaven. That's only fair."

"Good *things*?" said Randolph. "What about bad *thoughts*? Didn't Jesus say that looking at a woman lustfully was the same thing as committing adultery?"

"How is a person supposed to control their thoughts," asked Simone, "when they come right in like uninvited guests?" And sometimes never leave, she wanted to add. Ever since she had been a little girl she'd had a house full of unwanted voices in her head. That's why she tried not to think too much, why she sometimes had to drown them out. She'd learned at an early age that whiskey silenced the voices—at least for a little while.

"We must take every thought captive." The words slipped from Violet's mouth before she could stop them.

"Take thoughts captive?" Simone looked at Violet. "I'd say it's the other way around."

"I know what you mean," Violet said. "But Mama says our thinking is just one of our bodily functions; our thoughts don't define who we are. We need to take charge of them."

"What else does Mama say," Randolph said, amused. "And where do thoughts come from, now that we're getting into the metaphysical?"

"I don't know what you mean by *metaphysical*," Violet said. She wasn't afraid to admit she didn't know all of his fancy words. Most of the time she was confident that she knew what she believed, even if she didn't have big words to explain it. And this was a subject Mama had taught her over and over. "But thoughts can come from three places— God, the flesh, or the devil."

"Ha," said Randolph. "She shows her true color. Do you honestly believe that devil stuff?" He stuck his fork into a canned peach. The thick syrup dripped on the table in front of him. "I suppose you cater to the theory of fallen angels as well. Lucifer's army. Dante's inferno. Hellfire and damnation. The seven mortal sins. Here's to gluttony!" He stuck the peach in his mouth and grinned.

"Surely you believe in right and wrong," Violet said.

"What's the difference between Yahweh who rescues

his people by killing off the Egyptians' firstborn, and Molech who makes crops grow when the Ammonites sacrifice their babies to him?"

Simone felt the blood drain from her face. Suddenly she remembered that thing in the toilet upstairs and the bloody black sheets on her bed. How many times had it happened in just seven months of marriage? Hadn't God punished her enough? She felt weak. She needed to lie down.

"So what *do* you believe?" Violet asked Randolph. How did a person like him put his world together? He was a contradiction to her: talented and strong, yet cunningly wicked. He drew her like a moth to a flame. "Do you think we live in a godless universe?"

"The universe is godless, but not powerless," he said. "I've seen the power. Haven't you? How our thoughts become reality; how by wishing for something we can make it come true?"

"Not always," Simone said, almost in a whisper. It never seemed like she got what she wanted, not what she really wanted deep inside. She'd longed for Toby, not this cold life in the north.

"You have to know how to handle the power," Randolph went on, "how to tame it like a wild horse. You feed it, pet it, coax it into your yard, and win its trust. Then you can slowly slip a bit in its mouth and a saddle on its back—and ride away. Make it take you where *you* want to go. Harness the power of the universe for your own purposes."

"Sounds like the Atom Bomb," Violet said, "harnessing the power of the universe."

"Exactly," he said. "The atom is part of 'god' as you call

it. We're all part of God. The farther we evolve and advance through scientific knowledge, the more we can control."

"Control or destroy?" Violet said. "What about people killed by those bombs. Or the ones who had their limbs blown off…."

Simone's head dropped forward as she let out a moan.

Violet jumped up from her chair. "Miss Simone, you're white as a ghost. Let me help you to your room."

"No. I'm fine." She brushed off Violet's assistance. "I just didn't sleep well last night. I need a little nap." She stood and made her way round the table and out to the front of the house. Randolph and Violet waited in silence until they heard the sound of her door closing.

"Strange," Randolph said. But what he was really thinking was that Simone was strangely like his mother.

"Not so unusual for her," Violet said, remembering Ambra's trips to Simone's bedroom with trays of special food and the clandestine loads of laundry. Ambra never told Violet what went on up there—Ambra had the same kind-hearted loyalty as Mama—but Violet recognized the worry in her eyes and the concern in her voice whenever she spoke of Simone.

"But she hardly touched her meal," he said. "Is she sick?"

"She eats like a bird. Look at the size of her."

"No thinner than you." He raised his eyebrows. "In fact I'd say you two were nearly identical in size."

She felt his eyes focused on her like an animal watching its prey. Was this his way of telling her he had seen her in the window yesterday, dressed in Simone's nightgown? Or maybe he had measured them both with the grip of his long fingers. She didn't want to know.

"But we're not the same," she said. "I eat everything on my plate and still feel hungry. Hard work keeps me thin, not nerves."

"You think she's nervous?"

"I think you're asking too many questions. If you'll clear the table, then I'll wash up. Be sure to let me know if you get a door open to the outside. Until then I'll take my afternoon off in my room after all." Violet turned from his gaze, intent on finding some quiet time for herself. She needed to get away from these people with their depraved view of life. She needed to calm her own nerves.

*After separating the two halves of the house, the house mover
descends into the basement to build a system of four-by-four
foot cribs, like stacks of Lincoln logs, just shy of the floor joists.
Where the chimney and fireplace enter the house, the mover
makes a cross pinning out of steel plates so they cannot
topple down.*

Chapter 31

THIS IS NO FUN, thought Randolph after Violet closed
her bedroom door, leaving him alone in the kitchen. He'd
already done his time at the piano in the morning and he'd
stumbled on enough props—the pink slippers and the
mysterious love letter—for fun later on. Or had he? Was
there something more he could conjure up to make sure
the evening's conflagration would be hot enough to melt
the ice? Wasn't three the perfect number?

He looked out the kitchen window. The ice-covered
snow was a wedge nearly four feet high against the door.
But his eye was drawn to the garage. A feeling rose up in
him, a hunch, as if a voice were calling him, *Come to the
garage.* Something was in there. He had to go see. But how
could he get out? And if he did, the girls would expect him
to stay in his own rooms tonight. That would be no fun.

But if he could sneak out and back in again without being seen—that was a worthy project for this afternoon. Quietly he walked through the first floor surveying the rooms. Dining room, living room, study, front vestibule, library, sunroom, porch. All the windows and doors were blocked with snow. He almost gave up hope, but on his way back to the kitchen he had a bolt of inspiration: there was a secret cupboard under the bench next to the fireplace that had been built to store wood. It had an opening into the living room and also to the outside. Mrs. B told him she had stopped using it when the Scholar's Garden enclosed the entrance to the cupboard inside its walls. His pulse quickened. This was getting interesting. He went and stood on the bench and looked through the small leaded window above it. The walls of the garden had worked with the wind to create a small hollowed out space in the corner where the cupboard door opened. He stepped down from the bench and bent to look inside. Only a few yellowed newspapers and some kindling blocked his way. He had to hold back his excitement as he dashed to the mudroom to retrieve his boots and gloves and coat.

The clock struck one. If luck stayed with him he would have plenty of time to get out and back before Simone woke from her nap or Violet came out of her room to fix dinner. He buttoned his coat and pulled on his boots, then lay on his back on the living room floor with his feet inside the cupboard. He pushed hard against the outer door and it opened with a swoosh to a shower of bright snow. He turned around and onto his belly, pulled on his wool hat, and wriggled headfirst through the opening, out into an almost blinding light of silvery ice and snow. Standing up, he braced himself against the wall of the garden. Tall shoots of bamboo lined the corner by the house. He found that if he was careful he could plant his feet flat on the crusty surface and not break through. Perfect. No telltale tracks.

The garden was a scene from a science fiction novel. The large boulders that had been placed artfully along the path were now bulbous humps of snow. The winter plum—Mrs. B had told him it symbolized rebirth—was bent low to the ground under its white burden and looked more like a tomb than a sign of resurrection. The arched bridge that spanned the man-made stream was packed to its railings with snow. Ice coated the slat work of the small gazebo perched over the pond. He wondered if the fancy fat goldfish were still alive under all this winter weather. He made his way to the moon-shaped doorway, ducked down, and emerged in the back yard. The round doorway was hidden from external view by a row of Dwarf Siberian Pine. Mrs. B had thought of everything for her authentic Chinese garden. He laughed as he remembered the name she had given it—copied from her favorite garden in Suzhou—*The Three True Friends of Winter*. What had she had in mind? Wind, sun, and snow? Today it could be Randolph, Violet, and Simone.

Straight ahead of him was the huge Bur Oak. Snow piled up nearly to the top of the bench that encircled it. It was wonderful to be outdoors after such a storm. Everything was crisp and clean. And the sound—it was pristine, just birds chirping and the scuttle of squirrels, and a distant thrunch of snow dropping in the cedar woods across the field. If he had a singing voice, he'd bellow out the Hallelujah Chorus, it was that beautiful. He stepped on the circular bench and looked down the hill toward the road and the river beyond. Not one car or truck was in sight. Just like they said on the radio—everyone was staying home.

He jumped down and crashed through the icy crust. The snow came over his boots and nearly to his knees. When he tried to step up onto the surface, more crust broke under his weight. What had he heard about getting up onto ice if you fell through frozen water? Lincoln and his pals, the Spooks,—Randolph had pilfered through Lincoln's desk one day and found a stack of invitations to their secret powwows—had regular outings on the river and he'd overheard them talking about falling through at a sluice. Lay on your belly and swim onto the ice doing the breaststroke, someone said. So he flopped down gently on the crust and slithered forward, away from the hole he'd made. It worked. He stood and cautiously slid one boot in front of the other, careful not to slip, until he made his way to the garage.

He'd worked up quite a sweat and the sun was unforgivingly bright, so he unzipped his jacket and took off his red wool hat and stuck it in his pocket. To be on the safe side he went to the far end of the garage, out of sight from the house, to the small door underneath the stairs that led to his apartment. The stairway was solid with snow and slick with ice. The bright south sun was creating icicles along the roof and dripping them off the bottom on the stairs. They were too treacherous to climb; he'd have to forego clean underwear and his razor. Let Violet tease him about being a bear of a man. Today he was a polar bear.

He sized up the drifted mound blocking the garage door. Not too bad. The stairs had curtailed the wind. Besides, the door opened inward. In a minute he was inside.

Mrs. B's Studebaker stood in its stall next to Mr. B's Cadillac. Randolph had chauffeured them to the train station at the start of their trip. He was glad he'd had the sense to park his truck in Lincoln's spot when the storm started. He stopped and looked around. The trash bin next to Lincoln's stall drew his attention.

The bin was nearly empty, only a few things down at the bottom. It was one of Randolph's duties to collect the trash. He reached in past an empty windshield-washer fluid container, an oil can, half a dozen blue paper towels that smelled of Gojo. Old Lincoln was fastidious when it came to automobiles. Then his hand hit gold: a tidy packet of folded papers. He brought them up and spread them open on the workbench, catching light from the window. One piece was a hand-drawn map leading north from Chicago to a house in Lake Forest. Number 23 North Lane. At the bottom was a note in familiar handwriting. *The back door will be unlocked. Or I'll meet you under the apple tree! V.* Randolph let out a hoot for joy. Just as he thought, there was more than one V in Lincoln's life. And that bad boy was thrusting his hand through more than one latch opening. Randolph tucked his newest treasure inside his shirt and retraced his path back to the house.

Chapter 32

As soon as the kitchen was clean, Violet hung up her apron—the last vestige of servitude—and sped to her room. She wished the lock on her door really worked. She wanted to be in a space that was all her own, with no interruptions. Knowing Randolph, he'd try to get her involved in some sort of tomfoolery, or steal another kiss. She tried to put that image out of her mind—to take that thought captive, as her mother would say—but part of her wanted to linger there, to recall again the soft brush of his mustache and the warm pull of his lips. Even the smell of him, all clean and soapy last night as she lay sprawled for a moment against his chest, haunted her like a melody.

No! She clapped her hands in front of her as if the memory was a pesky mosquito she could rid from the room. She wouldn't let herself think about Randolph and the attraction she felt toward him. If she did, she'd have to admit where those thoughts—and feelings—came from. She wasn't ready to do that, to make it so black and white. Instead she'd practice self-control like her Mama was always saying. She'd put her mind on things above, or at least on things higher than sex.

Violet loved her room. All the furniture was painted sea-green, and had odd little designs on it. "It's called Tole," Mrs. B. had said in her low, raspy voice. "I painted it myself." Mrs. B wore a matter-of-fact confidence fashioned from a lifetime of affluence. The dresser had five drawers and when Violet first moved in last September, she never imagined she would fill all that space. Her few clothes fit in the top three, since her uniforms hung in the closet next to her hand-me-down winter coat. But now, only six months later, the bottom drawers were filled with treasures. She'd started a fine collection of smooth stones from the river across the road. She was hoarding a bundle of curled up birch bark. She wanted to make a little box for Mama like the one on Mrs. B's dressing table that had designs woven into the top with porcupine quills. Before Christmas she'd fashioned a wreath from bittersweet, and now the orange berries had shed their red shells into the corner of the drawer. She had a scattering of feathers, a bluebird's nest she'd found at the base of a tree in the orchard, and some giant pinecones gooey with sap that made the whole drawer smell fresh and free. Her most prized possession so far was an owl's pellet, a tightly matted mass laced with mouse fur and tiny mouse bones. It was like a miniature tomb, an airborne version of Jonah inside the whale, only this mouse hadn't been spit out on the shore to make peace with its enemies. It had been consumed.

She cleared off the top of her dresser and retrieved her Bible from the closet. She had a box full of odd pieces of felt and ribbon and various colors and shapes of sequins and beads left over from Mrs. B's many projects. She opened a manila envelope where she kept special pieces of paper she had torn from the blank parts of cards and letters thrown out by the Blankwells. She had several plain envelopes that had arrived inside wedding invitations. It troubled her to see such fine and expensive things going to waste.

She opened her jar of glue and took up the sharp pair of scissors she'd borrowed from the darning basket. Easter was only three weeks off and she was going to make cards to send to her family. She missed them all so much. She missed the smell of collard greens and black-eyed peas and the sound of the pot-belly stove crackling. Their house was always full of children—her little brothers and cousins and neighbors. Someone would be braiding corn rows, everyone would be singing or humming, with the old men clapping while they rocked on the porch. And Mama would be calling out words of kindness to whoever passed by. *Come on in, brothers and sisters, everyone's welcome. Hot corn bread on the griddle.*

She lost herself in the work. But it wasn't work to her; it was joy. She arranged her pressed flowers—apple blossoms, forsythia, honeysuckle, pink and white and purple flox—into bright designs and surrounded them with pressed leaves. She used tiny flowers—forget-me-nots and bits of Queen Anne's lace—to make the shape of a cross or to spell out the first letter in one of her family member's names. Almost two hours went by before the sound of Randolph at the piano stirred her from her reverie. He was playing something light and airy. She cleaned up her mess and set her Bible on top of the decorated cards to keep them from curling.

Now what should she do? She longed to go outside, to feel the sun shining on her face. Her room on the northeast corner of the house was already in shade. Had Randolph been able to get one of the doors open? She didn't want to ask him right now, didn't want to break the peaceful spell that was upon her. She remembered the empty master bedroom upstairs that faced full south. She could take her Robert Frost up there and read awhile before it was time to start dinner. She went through the pantry into the dining room directly below Simone's room and listened. Although the house had thick walls, the floors must have been poorly built because she could always track movement upstairs. Simone wasn't moving.

Violet ducked through the north end of the living room, avoiding Randolph at the piano, and carefully climbed the big front stairs. She slipped into Mr. and Mrs. Blankwell's bedroom but hesitated to close the door—it might look suspicious if Simone walked past—so she went further in, to the dressing room, which was also flooded with sunlight, and shut that door. It always struck her as such an odd room; the pink wallpaper swirled hydrangeas over every wall and even the ceiling. The doors to the closets— also wallpapered—were practically invisible, but she knew that behind them were shelves and rods of neatly folded or hanging clothes, enough for a dozen lifetimes. Enough for her whole home town. One thing she knew for certain: people might own every thing their heart desired, but that didn't mean they owned their own hearts. Just because the inside of their closet was tidy didn't say anything about the inside of their mind.

She stood in front of the window and closed her eyes, letting sun blaze red against her eyelids. She bowed her head and felt heat collect in her dark hair. There was a big patch of sunlight on the thick carpet. She couldn't resist. She sat down and let her whole body bathe in the light. Soon the mid-March sun did its penetrating work and she started to get warm. She took off her cardigan, then lifted her shirt to feel the touch of sun on her bare skin.

Violet's favorite time as a girl back home was always Sunday afternoons when she could steal away from the family commotion to a hidden glade in the woods behind their house where the tall grass had been tamped down by deer. She would step out of her Sunday clothes and peel off her underwear, then lie like a doe herself in the speckled sunlight. Those were the moments she felt closest to God, when his bright golden eye looked down upon her just the way he had made her. She felt beautiful in her berry brown skin. She was delighted to lie there and daydream, to be a natural part of the world like the birds gliding over-head and the squirrels chasing one another through the branches. With the sun on her skin, warm on her breasts, hot in the dark tangle of hair between her legs, she believed it was good to be a woman, good to be alive, that she was made for a purpose and one day she would know it just as the doe knew where to lay her young.

Through the floor she heard the piano rise and fall. Randolph was playing something slow and soothing. He sounded content. And only because she was certain he was occupied, she boldly did what she had been longing to do—she took off all her clothes and lay down in the sun. With her head cradled in her hands, she relaxed in the cocoon of warmth. No wonder people worshipped the sun. Such a powerful force beyond the earth. Without its light nothing could be seen. Without its heat nothing could live or grow. Had her ancestors in Africa worshipped the sun? The Egyptians did, the Egyptians who enslaved God's people in Africa. Then the tables turned and the Africans became slaves of white people—who thought they were God's *new* Israel. Where was God in all of this? What was skin color to Him? She knew what Mama would say. We're all from Adam and then, after the flood, from Noah. Moses married a Negro wife—so even the Lord Jesus had African blood in him. Now, Mama would say, we're slaves to Christ, not slaves to sin. Violet didn't want to be a slave to anyone.

She opened her eyes the tiniest bit and peeked through the hairs of her eyelashes. She imagined herself surrounded by tall jungle grasses. The music changed. Randolph began playing something low with an incessant bass beat. It was the lower part of the duet he had played with Simone before dinner the night before. The notes took her deeper into a warm, sub-Sahara sleep where she dreamed of wooden crosses adorned with flowers and wild antelope bounding across the Serengeti.

Chapter 33

SIMONE STIRRED IN HER SLEEP. In her dream it was a
hot afternoon on Swan Street. She lay on the porch swing
and drifted side to side as Toby picked out slow, sweet
melodies on his guitar. The music wrapped around her,
became Toby's fingers combing through her hair, tracing
the edge of her ear, trailing down her neck to the center
of her breast bone, cupping her breasts. She rolled over in
her bed. The dream shifted. It was a moonless night and
the big oak in the side yard at the Blankwells was hung
with Spanish moss that gradually turned into mistletoe.
Hideous little men in pointed hats climbed out of a hole
below the wooden bench that circled the tree. They stared
at her—she was lying on the grass—and chanted an eerie
dirge as they moved slowly toward her. They carried something between them on a stretcher—a tiny casket draped
with blood-red poppies. She tried to get up but something
was holding her leg, her ankle. She kicked at the sheets and
woke herself up, drenched in sweat.

She was in Lincoln's bed. She had taken her nap in

his bed because her own sheets were dirty and in the tub. Her foot had been pinned down in the corner because he insisted his bedding be tucked in tight as drum, like they did in the Navy. He always made her feel hemmed in. Then she remembered her dream. The awful men. The mistletoe. The muffled sound of the piano rose into her consciousness. Randolph was playing their duet again, the one he called the Dance of the Druids. If she didn't know better, she'd think he was trying to put a spell on her. Fortune telling, reincarnation. He acted like he knew her secret.

She sat up. She was famished. She'd hardly eaten lunch. A pot of tea and a plate of cookies were what she needed. She got out of bed and pulled her robe over her bra and panties and tugged on the braided cord that buzzed in the kitchen. She lit a cigarette and sat on the chaise waiting for Violet to come. A minute went by. Where was that girl? She waited a minute more, then got up and yanked the cord again. What was wrong with her? Violet had practically nothing to do on a day like this when Simone was the only one home. Except, of course, for Randolph who seemed to consider this his house too. She paced back and forth and lit another cigarette from the stub of the first one. She was starving.

She snubbed out her cigarette and went to the door. Did she have to yell down the stairs to get that girl's attention? She stepped into the hall and looked around. All was quiet; the music had stopped. Someone was walking about upstairs. She stood still and waited. Maybe Randolph *had* been sending her a message with that duet. Maybe he was coming to meet her. She tingled. She wouldn't mind a bit of cat and mouse.

She crossed the hall to the guest bath. She slipped the rubber bands off the ends of her braids and ran her fingers through her hair. She looked into the mirror, smoothing her robe down her hips and adjusting the overlap across her chest. She tightened the belt just a smidgen and waited behind the half-open door. He wouldn't expect her in there. She would surprise him.

But there was no sign of Randolph—or Violet. Enough of this tom foolery. Whoever was the fool, it wasn't going to be her. She sauntered down the hall and around the top of the big front staircase. Just beyond the window seat, through the open door into the master bedroom, Randolph stood with his back to her. She crept closer. Beyond him—and she could hardly believe this—Violet was kneeling on the dressing room floor with nothing but a skimpy shirt held up in front of her naked body. Simone screamed and ran down the hall, back to her room, and slammed the door.

When the cribs are in place under the floor joists, the mover
busts holes into the side of the foundation, lining them up
with the rows of cribs. He shreds bars of Ivory Soap, mixing
them with water into a mash of thick, slimy paste. He uses the
concoction to grease the tops of the cribs. Then he feeds heavy
I-beams through the holes, over the cribs, and out the other
side. Each I-beam sits on two or three cribs, depending on the
width of the house.

Chapter 34

THE HOUSE LAY QUIET AND STILL like a cat curled up in
the sun when Randolph shimmied his way back into the
living room through the secret passage next to the fireplace. He tugged off his boots and wrapped them inside
his coat so as not to leave any telltale drips on the way to
the kitchen. No need to tip off the girls. Violet had asked
to be told if he opened a door—not a cupboard. Ah, life
was good, electric with intrigue. He glanced lovingly at
the Steinway as he passed, his eyes still adjusting to the
interior darkness of the house. The piano keys shimmered
and blurred, black blending with white, as they caught
the corner of his eye. He couldn't wait to play with them

again: a dozen keys reaching out for his touch, wanting to be seduced, waiting to be conquered.

He replaced his coat on a peg in the mudroom, then sneaked one of Ambra's fig-filled cookies from the jar on top of the refrigerator. Tasty, but it didn't compare with a warm fig plucked fresh off a tree in France, hefty in the hand with its pasty pulp and bitter seeds. He loved to split open a fig with his thumbs and sniff the rank, sweet ripeness. The K-rations may have been paltry during the war, but the French countryside kept his senses satiated with wild fruit: tart cherries and blackberries in the spring, plump figs, and a dazzling array of grapes in the fall.

He padded back to the piano in his stocking feet and eased himself in front of the keyboard. The sweat from his exertion outdoors was beginning to dry; he felt a small chill. Carefully, cautiously he made contact with the keys. He closed his eyes, inviting the music to enter, to use him as a channel of its magic. A lullaby came forth, one his mother had played when he was a child. Perfect for the women in this house who he assumed were sleeping. His fingers fluttered over the keys, petting them, soothing them, mostly on the white ones, but then bending forward, stretching up just a bit to include the dark, minor ones. He loved the contrast, the dissonance, the tension, the resolution. The lullaby led him into a dreamy state. Soon thick bass strings begged to be thrummed. Their rhythm insistent, almost prophetic. Something was coming. Some dark power was demanding to be heard. He moved into the Dance of the Druids and played it over and over. He didn't need a partner; his hands were partners to one another. Sometimes the left took precedence and led. But then the high voice of the right hand wanted to be heard. His hands dueled, pranced, crossed over into the other's territory, mimicked one another in adjacent octaves, rushed to the crescendo, then ended with bravado at opposite ends of the keyboard.

Randolph slumped back and collected himself, like an octopus drawing in its legs. He didn't just make music; he made love to the piano. He caressed and pounded, thrust himself into the sound and felt the vibrations resonate in every layer of skin and muscle. Now his energy was spent, his mind calm, after the dizzying cascade of chords. He was acutely sensitive to any noise. Above him and a little toward the south, the floor creaked. Just a slight wooden groan followed by the softest plunk. Not a footstep; he recognized all the distinctive Blankwell treads: the rat-a-tat-tat of Mrs. B, the weary shuffle of her husband, Lincoln's unabashed striding. Simone wavered between tottering mania and a dragging depression—except when she was playing cat and mouse; then she could move almost as silently as he could. Randolph read the family like a simple musical score. Ambra was easy. She must weigh 200 pounds. Violet was more difficult, always conscious of herself and her surroundings. So who was moving upstairs in the master bedroom—or could it be the dressing room?

He held still and waited. Nothing more. But he knew he had heard something, something on the floor, not a piece of furniture. He couldn't stand not knowing; he had to investigate.

When he reached the top of the spiral staircase he saw that the master bedroom door was open and the room was empty, but the dressing room door was shut. Silently he crept through the bedroom and carefully turned the handle. The door opened in. He swung it wide and caught his breath: there lay Violet, naked and asleep in the sun, her skin smooth and brown as a beach. He drank her in, gulped her down. He traveled her contours, the rise of her breast, the dip to her waist, her broad hips and strong thighs. But his eyes kept returning to those darker places: the two dark coins and the hidden moss pressed between her legs.

The secret to a woman's beauty is found in the trinity; that's what his mother said. No! He didn't want to be thinking of that pale skin and fiery hair that had suffocated him on Louisiana afternoons when he was a boy. He looked back at Violet—so graceful, like a fawn in a hidden glade. He couldn't help himself; he reached out his hand and hovered over her breast. But his arm blocked the sun resting on her face and her eyes opened in his shadow.

Instantly Violet clutched her shirt and rose to her knees, covering herself the best she could. "How dare you?" she spit at him in a whispered voice. She didn't have the luxury of screaming.

But Simone did that for her. Or at her. Somehow she was there standing behind Randolph. Simone screamed and hell was loosed as she ran from the room, shrieking and cursing. Randolph jumped to his feet and was gone as fast as Simone.

Violet, now fully awake, pulled on her clothes. Her thoughts raced. She was completely humiliated. How could she have been so stupid? How could she have taken such a risk? Then she railed against Randolph: wicked, awful, lustful, lying, full of every abomination. She should never, ever, ever trust him again. And Simone—what a pitiful crazy drunk. Irrational, paranoid, and out to get her. What had she seen? What did she *think* she saw? What would she do? *O God,* she prayed in desperation, *O God, please help me.*

Chapter 35

RANDOLPH BANGED ON SIMONE'S DOOR. "It's not what you think," he said, wondering what she did think.

"Go away you brute," she yelled.

"Please, I want to explain."

"You play me for a fool," she said. "Go away this instant."

"Just give me a chance to explain. It's not what you think," he said again. "Something very wrong is going on here and I want to help you set things right." His words flowed from his mouth with almost no thought. It was as if he were watching himself talk. Like improvising on the piano. When he gave in to the emotions of the moment, his words tumbled out like music. He waited for Simone to answer. He sensed she was softening to him.

"Something *wrong*?" said her small voice.

"Terribly wrong, I'm afraid." He paused. "And I'm worried for you."

"For me?" She cracked open the door and peered out. His words and the look of earnestness on his face both calmed and frightened her. But she needed *someone's* help.

"Please," he said. "Can we talk?"

She opened the door and let him in. It was awkward having him in the bedroom, but she didn't know where Violet might be and Simon certainly didn't want to see her. "Sit there." She motioned to a chair next to the door. She picked up the cigarette case from beside her unmade bed and walked across the room to lean against the wall. Her watercolors, still lying on the window seat, reminded her that something had been wrong yesterday too. Terribly wrong. And getting worse.

She flicked the lighter and looked at him over the flame. "You have a lot of explaining to do, Randolph."

He watched as she took a deep drag, then blew smoke out the side of her mouth. Her braids were gone but her hair was kinked and sticking out at all angles. He'd never seen her look so disheveled—and her room was a terrible mess. Unmade beds were a hallmark of his mother. He waited, not speaking.

"So, what did you mean?" she said, breaking the silence. "How am *I* in danger?"

He looked at the floor to hide his grin. She was taking the bait.

"And exactly what was going on in that room over there?"

"I know that looked bad," he said with a shake of his head. "And it could have been bad, very bad. I'm so glad you rescued me." He gave her a look of gratefulness. "That Violet is a cunning woman. A real Jezebel."

Simone didn't know who Jezebel was—some woman from the Bible—but it sounded wicked. "So was she…was she trying to seduce you?" She whispered that awful word.

"She's *been* trying," he said wishing for a moment that it was true, wondering for just a split second what it would be like to really love someone like Violet. But the wheels of this drama were spinning too fast now to quit. He'd have to ride it through to the end. "I've been fighting her off behind the scenes for weeks. But lately she's become more aggressive. She seems to have a desperate need. And I'm afraid I'm not the only one she's after." He looked at her as the words sank in. Simone gave a gasp. He continued. "I should have come to you right away. I wasn't sure of my place. I didn't know if you'd believe me. But now I see how vulnerable you are. I've got to do the right thing to protect you, no matter the consequences to myself." He was amazed how the script was practically writing itself.

"What are you getting at?" She leaned toward him.

"I have no proof, but I've been noticing a lot of little signs. Now I'm afraid things have already gone too far. Yesterday…." He paused, not sure if he should play one of his trump cards.

"Yesterday what?" She was craning forward like a hungry seal at the zoo. If he tossed her this bit of truth, she'd swallow it whole.

"When I drove up the driveway yesterday afternoon—just as the storm was starting—I saw Violet standing in that very window next to you." Now he was on surer footing since he was telling the truth. "And she was *not* dressed in her uniform. I presume, though of course I wouldn't know, that what she was wearing was one of your negligées. You know you two are the same size."

Simone choked on her cigarette. Smoke plumed out

her nose. He would have laughed had he not been so intent in his deceit.

"Dressed in *my* nightgown?"

"And then later on, when I believe you were in the bath, I saw her in your mother-in-law's kimono." He laughed to himself. Violet *was* a bad girl.

"How horrible," she said. "How shockingly dreadful and impudent. The thought of it makes my skin crawl."

"I understand how you must feel," he said, though he'd be happy to crawl over either girl's skin. "She obviously has some sort of fetish with your clothes. But if that were all it was, I wouldn't be so worried." He paused to heighten the drama. Simone was a sucker for that sort of thing, a kitten lapping milk from his palm.

"Worried? Why?" She left her spot by the window and crossed the room to stand in front of him.

"It's hard to say this," he began. "I don't want to upset you, Miss Simone." He was thinking fast. It wasn't time to show his whole hand. He'd toss her another card or two and then sit out a round. "I don't know what she's done *to*, or *with* Mr. Lincoln, but I'm quite sure there's something very sick about her thinking. She doesn't know her place in this house. She's confused about who she is. The truth of the matter is," he didn't flinch at all over the word truth, "it seems like Violet wants to replace you."

"Replace me? That's ludicrous. She's nobody. She's just the maid."

"I know, I know," he said as if to reassure her. "I think there's something fundamentally wrong with her mind. You already know about her twin sister...." He let that thought hang in the air.

"Oh God," she said. "You really think so?"

He just nodded.

"And you think she might be dangerous? That I might be in danger?"

He stood up, just a few inches from her. "It's too bad there's no way to get out of the house tonight. And the phone isn't working. But at least I'm here." He opened his palms toward her in a gesture of offering himself.

"Oh Randolph. We've got to stick together." She almost took his hands, wishing she could lean against his chest, but even she knew that wouldn't be wise.

"I'll go down and have a talking to her. When you're ready to confront her—to put her in her place—give me a sign and I'll be right there by your side."

Chapter 36

VIOLET SAT IN HER ROOM MORTIFIED. She didn't know what was worse—being seen naked *by* Randolph, or being seen naked *with* Randolph. She could only imagine what thoughts were going through Simone's head. That girl was so unstable. This might push her to the breaking point. She'd jump to conclusions, get paranoid, and one thing Violet knew for sure, Simone would blame everything on her. This would be the end. The train ticket would take all her savings, but soon she'd be back in Missouri. Mama would be so disappointed, yet Mama would understand. Mama loved her.

She took comfort in the thought that Mama knew her through and through. She knew Violet's curiosity and the way she loved pretty things. Mama understood the joy of opening your body to the elements—she was the one who took Violet skinny-dipping in the creek on moonlit nights. And Mama knew she was a good girl at heart. She wouldn't hurt anyone on purpose. She wouldn't fool around with men, especially not white men. Mama believed that, didn't she? Violet was wondering what she knew about herself. Was she really bad? Where was her self-control? She had been just as shocked as Randolph the night before when she slapped him in the kitchen. And she didn't know what came over her when she pushed the plate of strawberry shortcake into Simone's face. It must be this trapped-in feeling that made her lash out like that. She had to watch herself more carefully from now on.

From now on. Those words seemed impossible. What was she going to do? How could she carry on with her duties? But she must. She slipped out of her corduroys and cardigan and changed into her uniform. That would help. No more pretending she was one of them. She would keep her eyes low and do exactly what was required. She would speak only when spoken to. Besides, Simone would probably hide in her room until tomorrow. She could handle Randolph face to face now that she had no doubts about what kind of man he was.

She heard heavy footsteps coming down the back stairs—Randolph—and finished tying her apron as he rapped on her door.

"Violet, it's me. I've come to apologize."

She set her jaw and opened the door.

"May I come in?"

"No you may not." She avoided looking at him. He didn't deserve her attention. She walked past him and into the kitchen. He followed.

"I was way out of line. I had no right…"

"You certainly didn't." She stopped at the sink and turned to look at him. She could easily imagine catfish spines sticking out of his back; he was just that slimy and cruel.

"I beg your forgiveness," he said, hanging his head in a repentant pose. "It's just that I was trying to find you, and then when I did, I was taken aback by your beauty..."

She cut him off. "Just shut up. You've done enough harm. There's nothing between you and me and if you care for me at all, as you claim you do, then quit your games and tell Simone the truth—that what she saw was you breaking into *my* privacy." When she said the word truth she knew that was her only hope. If she told the truth, then she'd be free, no matter what.

"You're right, it was all my fault," he said. "I shouldn't have opened the door without knocking." The words slid from his lips. He knew what she wanted to hear. He was a performer, after all. An improviser. "I tried to tell that to Simone just now..."

"You've been talking to her?"

"I thought it best to see if I could calm the waters. But I'm afraid she's made up her mind, despite the truth."

"I know I've lost my job. I deserve to be fired after what I did last night."

"I'm afraid it's more than that." He used his big brother tone. "She has it in her mind that you've been playing some kind of hanky-panky with Lincoln. And that's why he left, to escape your advances."

"What? That's crazy." He held up his hand as she shook her head in disbelief.

"She's convinced herself that you're mentally unstable. She even mentioned something about your sister. That your whole family is mentally ill—and dangerous."

"My sister? She's not dangerous; she's just slow. And the rest of us are—well that's an outright lie."

"The Blankwells are powerful people, Violet. You know that by now. They always get what they want."

"And what do you think Simone wants? Surely she can't believe I've been fooling around with her husband?"

"From what she just told me, she wants to have you arrested. Have Rosie put away. She wants to destroy you *and* your family. Completely."

"My family? No!" Violet nearly shouted. "It has nothing to do with them." Fear gripped her heart. "What can I do? I have to protect them. You're the only one who knows the truth. You've got to help me."

God helps those who help themselves, he thought as he stepped forward and cradled her head against his shoulder. He was determined to help himself to one of the women, he didn't care which one. He figured by tomorrow the doors would open, Lincoln would be home, and his chance would be long gone. If something was going to happen, it had to be tonight.

"I'll do whatever I can," he said patting her back. "Don't worry, everything will turn out right." He glanced up at the box where the buzzer system signaled a call and saw that Simone's room was highlighted. Carefully he reached over with his free hand and pressed the button to undo the call. He didn't want the two women to see each other just yet. "I'm sure she'll settle down," he said, "like she did last night. Just keep your distance for now. I'll take care of everything." He let go of her. After all he was just being a protective big brother.

Chapter 37

THE NEXT HOUR IN THE HOUSE WAS QUIET. Randolph lit a fire and settled into Mr. B's chair with his pipe in his mouth and a book about French architecture on his lap. Upstairs Simone sat on the windowsill and stared out her bedroom window, watching the sun set over the river, numbing herself with cigarettes and the remainder of her W. B. Yeats. Her thoughts were in a knot. She felt like she couldn't move. She was frozen in time. No one was there for her. Maybe she didn't even exist. She had taken the wrong turn somewhere in her life. She had mistaken Lincoln's smooth manners for affection and followed him north to this icy house where he had deposited her like an old photo album that he could pick up and thumb through when he was bored.

She left the window and stood in front of the mirror. It was nearly dinnertime and she wasn't even dressed. She was disgusting. She opened the edges of her robe and looked at herself. Her small breasts hung sad and pale like withered blossoms. She could see her ribs and the hollow between her hips. Randolph had said something about how she and Violet were the same size—but Simone felt like a shadow compared to the strong brown body she'd just seen.

But she was the one in charge here, she must never forget that. She must take charge of herself, and take charge of the house. Randolph said he'd help her, and that's what he'd better do. He was the handy man, after all. She flung open her closet and pulled out a pair of wool slacks. She'd wear those and her rosey cashmere sweater. No one would be confused about who was whom.

She brushed her hair back and made one thick braid down her back—that always made her look older—and went downstairs to meet Randolph at the piano.

Violet was busy in the kitchen making a quick batch of blueberry muffins. She'd poach eggs and fry up some corned beef hash. That was one of Simone's favorite suppers. They all needed an early dinner and a quiet evening. Maybe she could postpone her talk with Simone until after a good night's rest.

She set the table for three— she didn't want to upset Simone even more by excluding her—though God knew she hoped they could each eat alone. The hash was frying and the egg water was at a boil when she heard the creak of the front stairs. She reminded herself that her place was in the kitchen. She should only go elsewhere when she was called.

The piano sounded, tentatively at first. It was a simple, melancholy melody. *Blue Moon*. It must be Simone. She often played that song. Now bass chords were added.

Was Simone playing the whole thing or were they playing a duet? She listened carefully for a moment and heard the syncopated flourish that only Randolph could add. Was he talking to her? She'd like to know. She'd like to see what sort of state Simone was in before she had to confront her.

When Simone had come downstairs and started playing the duet, Randolph knew that was his cue to go to her. She'd relaxed quite a bit since he'd talked to her in her room. She'd combed her hair and put on a cozy sweater. Once he sat down next to her at the piano he didn't have any trouble convincing her to eat in the kitchen. "We'll act as normal as possible," he told Simone. "That way Violet won't get agitated. We don't want her to do anything irrational. At the first hint of danger, I'll back you up. Don't worry." They finished the song and went to the kitchen together. "Smells good in here, doesn't it?" Randolph said to Simone in a tone one would use with a child.

Simone said nothing.

"Violet's been doing a good job of feeding us, hasn't she?" He escorted Simone to the table, staying right by her side.

Simone took a seat. "Blueberry muffins. I'm famished."

Violet slid eggs into simmering vinegar water and turned toward the table. Should she speak? Apologize? For what? She hadn't really done anything wrong, except to be in Mrs. B's room. She would wait. She was used to being invisible.

She glanced over her shoulder at Simone. She was dressed in slacks and a fancy sweater, with her hair in one short braid down her back. Despite her choice of clothes, she looked like a little girl. She was a little girl, a scared and insecure girl. Violet felt a pang of compassion for her. Simone was the one who was trapped here, not her. This was Simone's *family*, not just a job. And from all Violet observed, Simone wasn't treated with any more respect— maybe even less—than the servants. It was too bad they couldn't have been friends. She set the basket of muffins on the table in front of her.

"Thank you," Simone said. "Is that corned beef hash I smell?"

"Yes, Ma'am. Would you like one or two eggs?"

"Two for me. How about you, Randolph?" They were acting awfully friendly. Maybe that was good. Maybe he had talked some sense into her.

He looked from one woman to the next. "Would four be too greedy? Four softly poached eggs, two on each side of a big slab of corned beef hash?"

Violet blushed and fixed their plates, brought them to the table, and sat down.

"I'll say grace tonight," Simone said with just a quick glance in Violet's direction. She was reasserting her role as head of the house. She folded her hands and said, "For the blessings we are about to receive, may we be eternally thankful."

"Amen," Randolph said and reached for the salt and pepper.

"Was that right?" Simone said, her fork suspended in the air in front of her. "Eternally thankful? Or is it forever grateful?" She looked at Violet. "You've heard Mrs. Blankwell say grace. What does she say?" Her words were slightly slurred.

"It was just fine, Ma'am," Violet said. "It's the sentiment that counts."

"No, it wasn't *just fine*. Don't give me that. What does Mrs. Blankwell Sr. say?"

"I'm quite sure it's eternally thankful, isn't it, Randolph?" She turned to him. There was a queer glimmer in his eye.

"Don't get me in the middle," he said. "I don't eat in the dining room. I don't overhear their prayers. I haven't been eavesdropping on the Blankwells."

Violet looked at him. What was he doing?

He continued. "I know where I belong and where I don't. I know *my* place."

"Like at the *grand* piano?" Violet fell in his trap.

"An empty living room can hardly be compared to a private bedroom—or dressing room." There, he had loosed the tide. He had set the course. Now Simone could take the helm. What did the Bible say? Words were like a tiny rudder; it only took a few of them to steer a big ship.

"Randolph!" Violet said. Why was he betraying her?

"I hardly think you should blame him," Simone piped in. "You're the one who was lying naked in my mother-in-law's private dressing room." She splayed her fingers flat on top of the table. "You're the one who put on her kimono—after I had been wearing it." Simone's voice got higher and louder with each sentence. "And you're the one," she stood up and pointed a long bony finger in Violet's face, "who stood in *my* window wearing *my* wedding night negligée. I can only guess what other depravity has been going on right under my nose—and under my sheets!" She ended with a screech and ran from the kitchen, straight up the back stairs, and slammed her door.

"You snake," Violet hissed at Randolph.

He laughed. "The truth hurts, doesn't it Violet."

She turned from him, leaving the half-eaten food on the table, and ran to her room.

On to round three, Randolph said to himself. The night was still young.

Chapter 38

THE TENSION WITHIN VIOLET tossed her back and forth like a small ship at sea, riding up the crest of compassion, then sinking deep into a trough of guilt. Randolph's betrayal was a sharp arrow of truth that pierced her flimsy raft of self-righteousness. It drove her down, under water, and pinned her to the bottom. She felt like she was going to drown.

Randolph had betrayed her, but Simone was right: she couldn't blame him. She was the one who had given in to the temptation of beautiful clothes—the lust of the eyes. She had tried on Simone's identity and now the girl's crazy paranoia was clinging to her like a second skin. The game was over and Violet had lost.

Should she start packing? She looked around her room. It wouldn't take more than half an hour to fold the things that belonged to her and put them in her satchel. What she needed most was a breath of fresh air. There had to be some way to get outside. She went to her window. The snow reflected a pale lavender from the sinking sun. The air must be warming—a slight fog hung a few inches above the ground. Most of the ice had melted from her window and dropped off the sill.

She climbed on her bed and scooped her collection of colored glass and stones off the windowsill and stashed them under her pillow. She turned the latch on the top of the window. It slid up easily. Then she fiddled with the old storm window. They didn't have storm windows back home and she wasn't sure how it was attached, but after a moment or two of jiggling and pounding, the bottom came loose, and as she pushed it out away from the house the whole thing fell with a swoosh into the snow bank below. She was free. Soft air rushed into her room carrying the southern scent of home. Maybe the storm was over for good.

Luckily her coat and boots were in her own closet. Mrs. B said she and Ambra needed to keep their things in their rooms or the mudroom would become a frightful mess. Wasn't that the point of a mudroom? But now she was glad of it. She didn't risk running into Randolph or Simone.

She climbed back on her bed, boots in hand, then stuck her feet out the window and pulled the boots on. She had better manners than to muss the spread, even if she would be gone tomorrow and never have to wash it again. She got the top of her body out the window, perched on the sill, then pushed herself out, away from the storm window, and into the snow. She landed with a soft plop in a mound of snow blanketing the thick euonymus that edged the corner of the house. The air was still and cottony soft. The waning moon hung low in the southern sky. She listened closely and could make out the tinkling of the river down the hill.

She'd love to walk over and look for the tracks of animals on their way to drink, but crossing the front yard would expose her to too many windows. Also, the pear orchard was in Simone's sight line. She decided to go around the garage and head out to the cedar woods to see how the owls and squirrels had weathered the storm.

With every step she sunk deep into snow. It came up over her boots, but she'd thought to pull her corduroys on under her uniform, so her legs and feet stayed dry. She passed the woodpile. It looked like an old dwarf laboring under a heavy load. She couldn't make out the driveway; the drifting snow had refashioned the landscape to its own liking. She stayed to the outside of the garage. When she was sure she was hidden from view of the house, she ran along the edge of the field, kicking up snow and bending down to scoop up handfuls, then threw a hard ball high into the air. She longed to fly like a hawk over woods and fields, to trace the secret meanderings of rivers and streams, to get a heavenly perspective. She would understand life better if she could just rise above it for awhile.

Her walking slowed as she approached the woods. She was exhausted. The cedars looked tired themselves, their branches bent low with the weight of the snow. She stepped under the outer trees and unbuttoned her coat. All the traipsing had made her sweat. She passed from tree to tree, holding onto their straight trunks, dodging stray branches. The trees were her friends. She imagined them to be stately columns in a grand palace where she was always welcome. But suddenly everything changed. The ground was dry. Wind and snow had not driven through the branches in this part of the woods and not a speck of light penetrated the snow-packed branches above. No pale evening dusk found its way in from the outer edges because of the snow piled high around the perimeter of the woods. It was pitch black. Near absolute darkness, like the caves she'd visited in Kentucky. She felt as if she were inside a cedar box with the lid closed. An owl hooted. She shuddered. The friendly woods turned into a coffin. Panic overwhelmed her.

She thrashed through the trees, now a maze of trickery and deceit. It was so dark she couldn't see her hand before her face. She pushed on, trusting her sense of direction until she broke through the edge of the woods and into the open field where nothing blocked her from the wide eye of the sky. She stopped to breathe, her heart pounding. She'd better get back to her room and prepare herself for leaving.

She retraced her tracks along the edge of the field. The river valley below her was filled with mist. It mounted up the hill toward the house, moving stealthily like smoke from a fire. Just as she reached the edge of the garage she noticed something strange—snow had been dug away from the side door. Someone had been in there. Today. She knew who that someone was, that snake, that cheat. Now she could see the path he had taken. She followed it along the front of the garage and there in the snow, as dark as a pool of blood in the moonlight, lay his red wool hat. What a liar he was. She should march right in the house and show Simone how he had tricked them, making them think they were trapped in the house. She wouldn't be surprised if he had even cut the phone lines. But then she remembered she was in no position to talk to Simone about anything. Simone would never believe her. She would always be the guilty one, the one forever marked with the dark stain of Cain.

Even as she resigned herself to her fate she couldn't help wonder how Randolph had gotten out. None of the doors to the house—as far as she could tell—were open. She stuck his hat deep in her pocket and followed his tracks, barely visible as slight indentations on the surface of the crusty snow. The snow must have been firmer when he was outside. She scanned the yard and noticed a big hole near the oak tree bench. From there she traced his trail and found it led straight into the Scholar's garden and the wood box. He was a cunning trickster; she'd known that all along.

She found her way back to her open widow and with the strength she had gained from all her hard work, she hoisted herself up and tumbled head-first onto her bed.

*Under the I-beams the house mover sets up jacks and raises
the house until it is three feet above grade. He takes two
dollies—eight-wheeled contraptions with a short axle and
a saddle where the beam sits—and puts one on each side
of the house, near the back.*

Chapter 39

RANDOLPH FINISHED HIS EGGS AND HASH and cleared
the table. The least he could do for Violet was wash the
dishes. Besides, he knew women well enough to know that
they needed time to simmer down before he brought them
up to the boiling point again. That was one of the great
things about women—if a man knew what was what, he
could play with them like a yo-yo, up and down, always
getting them to come back to his hand wanting more. A
woman's desire was for the man, but he lorded it over her.
The curse of poor gullible Eve.

He switched on the radio and tuned in the Philco
Radio Time program. Judy Garland and Bing Crosby were
singing "*I've Got You Under My Skin.*" Ain't that the truth,
he thought. He listened to the weather report—the melt
was underway. His time was slipping away with the snow.

He wondered what his next step should be. He knew Violet was livid. He wouldn't be able to touch her with a ten-foot pole. But maybe Simone could use some comforting. He hung up the dishtowel and took out the bottle of wine he'd hidden behind the flour bin. It was an even better vintage than what they'd had the night before. He filled two glasses and left the rest of the bottle in the kitchen, then went up the front stairs.

"Simone?" he said as he tapped on her door, "I've brought you a little something to help you relax."

She opened the door at once and rushed him in. "You said you'd stick with me. I've been waiting up here for twenty minutes. Where have you been? Have you been talking to her?"

He handed her a glass. "Don't fret," he said. "She left the kitchen when you did. She's in her room. I've been cleaning up the mess she left and trying to get a door open so that you can stay in my apartment if you don't feel safe here." Where did that idea come from he wondered? He was a genius. Maybe he really should try to open a door.

"And did you have any luck?" She settled onto her chaise and pulled a blanket over her bare feet. He noticed for the first time that she had changed into a satin robe, midnight blue with lace appliqued over the shoulders. His thoughts wandered and she had to repeat her question. "The door—did you get one open?"

"Oh, sorry," he said. "They're dead shut with the weight of ice and snow. But I'll give it another shot later on. The radio says the temperature's rising—it's above freezing right now."

"What a relief. That means Lincoln should be able to

make his way home tomorrow." She drained the bottom of her glass. "I think I'll go see if the phone is working." She sprung from the chaise, revitalized.

"Good idea," he said. "And I'll go refresh our glasses." He followed her down the front stairs and went into the kitchen. He knew the telephone service was still off; they'd announced that on the radio. But why should he tell her?

"Still no operator," she said padding into the kitchen in her bare feet. "Ooh, the linoleum's chilly," she said, then she caught herself and whispered, "Where is she?"

"It's okay. She's in her room with the door shut." He showed her the label on the wine bottle. "Your father-in-law has good taste."

"Don't you know the hallmark of a Blankwell is good taste. Excellent taste. But the question is, do *they* taste good?" She laughed at her own joke. He could see she was getting tipsy. "Randolph, let's go play the piano again. Teach me a new duet." She liked to be alone when she drank vodka, but wine turned her into an extrovert. "Pretty please?"

"Sounds like fun," he said. "But shouldn't you put on some shoes?"

"Oh huff. You sound like Lincoln. I'll go barefoot if I want to." She started out into the hall.

He followed her to the Steinway, then played one of his trump cards. "But your feet looked so elegant last night in those pink satin shoes."

"See," she smiled, trailing her fingers along the smooth black surface of the piano. "You're a man of good taste too. Those are very expensive shoes."

"Hmmm," he said waiting.

"But now that I think of it, where are they? I know I was wearing them last night. I asked *her* about them this morning," she didn't want to say Violet's name, "and she pretended to know nothing at all."

"Really?"

"Oh my God, you don't think…?" She put her glass down on the piano lid.

"Under the circumstances, with all that's gone on, how can one not come to that conclusion?"

"I think I should wait until tomorrow and let Lincoln handle this."

"Yes, that's a wise idea," he said, letting his voice drop. "But if you had seen everything that I've seen…."

"What? What are you getting at?" Her face tightened up, ready for an explosion.

"Simone, I don't want to be the bearer of bad news, but if I were you, I'd look in her room for the shoes right now." He got another brainstorm. "In fact, I'll do it for you if you want me to."

"You're right. Let's face the music together." She grabbed his arm, strode through the kitchen, down the hall, and stopped in front of Violet's room. "You go in. I'll wait here."

He knocked loudly on the door. "Violet," he said with authority, "Simone is standing here with me and she insists that you open the door."

There was no answer. He turned to Simone and whispered, "You're the mistress of the house. She has to do what you say."

"You heard him," said Simone. "Open the door this instant."

There was still no sound, but cold air was seeping from

under the door. Simone grabbed the handle and opened it herself.

"Oh no!" she pointed to the open window. "She's escaped."

"I doubt that," he said, looking around. "All her things are here." He paused, then went to the closet. "All her things and some of yours. Look!" He motioned to the back of the closet, behind a cardboard box.

"My Ferragamos!" she cried. "I am so repulsed to think of her horrible colored feet in my precious shoes."

Randolph picked them up off the floor. "Maybe she didn't wear them. Maybe she was going to sell them."

"Nonsense," she said. "Give them to me. Of course she…. What's this? A letter?"

Randolph couldn't keep the grin off his face.

Simone was busy reading: "*To L from V.* You don't suppose?" She turned to him with shock. "*Kiss me with the kisses of your mouth…I have taken off my robe…he browses among the lilies.* This is a love letter!" She looked like she might faint.

He put his arm around her and she started to cry. He guided her out the room and up the back stairs. "What a terrible shock," he said. "I wanted to protect you." He plied her with all the comforting phrases he could think of until he thought of another tack. "But maybe she never gave the letter to him. Otherwise, why would it still be in her room?"

She stopped sobbing for a moment and looked at him. "You think so?"

"That's the only thing that makes sense."

"I know Lincoln would never dream of touching an animal like that."

"Of course not," he said. "It's all in her mind. Thank God you found the letter before it did more harm. I'm sure nothing's gone on between them. You've saved Lincoln from her clutches—just like you saved me."

They were at her door. "You go rest now," he said. "You're exhausted."

"I'll take a hot bath; that will help."

"I'll wait downstairs and keep guard in case Violet returns. I won't let her get close to you."

"Thank you, thank you, Randolph." She planted a quick kiss on his cheek. His wide mustache brushed her skin like a moth in the night. "Whatever would I do without you?"

He closed the door and practically skipped down the hall to the stairway.

Chapter 40

AS SOON AS VIOLET CLIMBED IN through her window, she sensed that something was different in her room. Had she left the closet door ajar? She had trained herself to check and double check all her moves. Mrs. B hated nothing more than gaping cupboard doors or half-closed drawers. But she had been upset and in a hurry before she climbed out the window. She must have forgotten to close it.

She shut the window quietly and hid Randolph's hat in the back of her closet. She changed out of her wet clothes and into her nightgown and robe. Surely her working day was over. The walk through the woods had made her tired and ready for sleep. That was one of the wonderful things about the outdoors—the strength and steadfastness of nature shrank her problems down to size. Nothing was too big for God; he would help her sort this all out in the morning. After she apologized and resigned her job, she would show the hat to Simone who would see that Randolph was a liar. But her bags would already be packed. She would walk to the train station and leave this life behind. She would make a fresh start. Mama would help.

Her nightgown was soft against her skin. Mama had made matching gowns for Rosie and her plus a set of curtains for their house—all from the end of a bolt of fabric Mrs. Applebaum had given her. It was a high grade of cotton but one edge had been damaged with water stains. Mama just cut that bit off and made do. It was a cheerful pattern with bright apples hanging from the branches of sturdy trees that were planted near a stream. Mrs. Applebaum, understandably, loved everything having to do with apples. Even her kitchen chairs had apples painted on the seats.

Violet held up the edge of the gown and rubbed the worn fabric against her lips. Simple things were best, she told herself. She sat on the edge of her bed and listened for sounds in the house. She had to make rounds before turning in. She'd put the dirty dishes to soak in the sink for tomorrow, but she must check the fireplaces and turn off the lights. She hoped she could do it without seeing anyone. Simone's slow footsteps crossed the floor of her room upstairs. There was no sound from Randolph. Maybe he was asleep. She wasn't sure how long she'd been outdoors. It felt like hours. She could tell by the faint shadows outside her window that the moon had dropped toward the western horizon. It must be after ten. She would sit in bed and read for awhile until all the noises of the house grew quiet.

Just as she was settling under the covers with Robert Frost an awful shriek rang out from upstairs followed by a string of angry shouts that could only be curses coming from Simone. By force of habit her feet were on the floor in an instant and she was almost to the door when she made herself stop. Was this her responsibility? Wasn't she the last person in the world Simone wanted to see tonight? Wasn't it likely that Randolph was already slithering up there on his lying belly?

This last thought jolted her more than the screaming. Maybe he *was* up there. Maybe he had taken his advances too far.

She grabbed her robe and went to the bottom of the stairs to listen. Just as she thought, it was Simone. Profanities were flying like hot grease spattering in a pan. As she stood in the kitchen doorway, the lights still on, she noticed the call indicator from Simone's room was highlighted. She braced herself—she'd better go up and see what was going on.

With every step up the steep back stairs her sense of dread grew. This was enemy territory. By the time she got there, Simone's door was closed and the shouting had stopped. She rapped firmly. "Miss Simone? Are you all right?" She used her best subservient voice.

The door flew open. Violet stared in shock, then lowered her eyes. Simone was half-naked and cradling a bloody mass of wet sheets in her arms. "Look," Simone said with a steely voice. "Look at this mess."

Violet glanced up but recoiled when she met Simone's eyes. They were like two black holes, two bottomless pits with demons glaring out at her. The words coming out of her mouth were straight from hell.

"You're as filthy as these bloody sheets, you whore," Simone spit. "You couldn't stop with wearing my clothes, could you?" Her mouth was like a pit of stinking sulfur. "Or stealing my shoes?" She glared at Violet. "You had to steal my husband too, you bloody whore."

Violet was dumbfounded. "I don't know what you mean," she cried. "I haven't stolen anything."

"*Kiss me with the kisses of your mouth…*" Simone said in her baby voice. "Is that some fancy metaphor?"

Clearly Simone was out of her mind. Violet knew the only way to handle her was like a child. "Here, let me take those sheets from you," Violet said to distract her. "I'll put them in the wash and get some clean ones right away."

"How dare you be so calm." Simone said. "You should have thought about that hours ago, you lazy bitch." There was that word Violet had hurled at Simone the night before coming right back at Violet. The word hissed from her lips like smoke from the abyss.

"I should have, Ma'am." There was no use in reminding Simone she had released Violet from her duties and said to leave her rooms until tomorrow. Violet took off her robe and wrapped it around the cold dripping mess. No sense having blood tracked all over the house. As she turned to leave Simone grabbed the sleeve of her nightgown.

"Not so fast." Simone's grip was strong. "Don't you want to know what you're carrying there, swaddled like some newborn babe?"

"Please Ma'am. We've all had a hard day. Let me make up your bed and we can talk in the morning. I know I've done things wrong, but there's more to the story than you know."

"Ha. More than I know? You'd be surprised what I know." She yanked Violet into her room and slammed the door. "You think I'm stu-pid. Everyone thinks I'm stu-pid. And ug-ly. Ug-ly." Simone's voice had a frightening sing-songy lilt. It was a voice of torment. "I can't even make a baby." As Simone's words sunk in, Violet shifted the bundle of sheets away from her body.

"Don't worry, its not in there. It's long gone, gone with the other two, down the toilet like the rest of the filth that comes out of me."

"A baby?" Violet said. "You had a baby?"

"Not really," Simone laughed. "Just a knotted wad of blood and guts. Like the other two."

"I'm so sorry," Violet said.

Simone laughed again, an eerie, high-pitched stage laugh. "*You're* sorry? I bet you're sorry. You're sorry he's not here tonight to creep down to your apple tree and thrust his hand through your latch."

Violet had no idea what she was talking about. "I am sorry for you, Miss Simone. So sorry about all the babies." No matter how much the girl hated her, Violet still felt pity.

"The babies? I'd hardly call them that. It's a good thing they're dead. Isn't that nature's way? There was some-thing wrong with them. If they'd lived, they'd probably be deformed retards like your sister. Or demented psycho-paths like you."

"Enough," Violet said and tried to pry her gown from Simone's clawed grip. "You can sleep in Lincoln's bed." She turned to leave but Simone lunged for the neck of the nightgown, and as they fought against each other she ripped open the front down to below Violet's belly, expos-ing her breasts and her dark triangle of hair. A piece of the fabric came lose in her hand. Violet clutched the torn gown and bloody bundle of sheets, trying to hide herself. She was stunned.

Simone laughed and dangled the cloth in front of Violet. "What's this? Your maidenhead?"

"Give that to me," Violet grabbed at the fabric.

Simone shrieked again, as loud as the first wild wail that had started the awful episode. "This is it," she said. "Here is all the proof I need. The apple tree." She was looking at the fabric. "It *is* you. You *are* the one, you vile slut. *Under the apple tree I roused you.* I hate you, I hate you, Violet. I hate you," she screamed. Then abruptly she stopped and took a deep breath. "And mark my words," she said in a low, menacing voice, "You won't get away with this. You are ruined forever. You and your *family.*"

Violet turned and ran from the room and down the back stairs.

Chapter 41

FROM HIS COMFORTABLE VANTAGE on the window seat at the top of the front staircase, Randolph was able to hear almost everything the two women said until something happened and the door slammed. Bloody sheets, lazy bitch, whore. Things were progressing better than he could have imagined. Simone had even quoted from the mysterious letter, though it was hardly mysterious to him. He knew the *V* in question wasn't sweet virginal Violet, but Lincoln's former fiancée from Chicago. He'd save the map he'd found in the garage trash can for himself, to spin into gold at a later date.

The grandfather clock struck eleven. He mused at how odd it was that though he'd been in this house for thirty-one straight hours—excepting his romp in the snow—he'd only noticed the bonging of the clock a handful of times. What was it about time that made it slow to a stagger during some parts of the day, and other times it moved so fast it seemed to disappear? Relativity. It must be that. The closest he could come to understanding physics was at the keyboard. He knew that when he played certain pieces, when he dropped from his mind into his body, time twisted and bent, it drew out like saltwater taffy, pressed together like a wisp of cotton candy, lost him in its never-ending maze. When an Old Testament priest went into the Tabernacle, into the Holy of Holies, the Law required a rope be tied around his foot so he could be pulled out in case he died on duty. Sometimes Randolph thought he needed a rope around him when he started to play. Especially the Mahler piece he was working on. He was transcribing parts of *Das Lied von der Erde*—"The Song of the Earth"—for the piano. It should have been called the Ninth Symphony, but Mahler was superstitious. Beethoven and Buckner both died after writing their ninths. But there's no fooling Fate. Mahler died before *Das Lied* was performed. The music was based on old Chinese poems and was a sweeping union of Christian mysticism and pagan pantheism. Right up Randolph's alley.

He sat perfectly still. Water gushed in the pipes—Violet filling the washing machine in the basement. He listened to her stirring embers in the fireplace and heard the thick chunk as she closed the damper. Lights downstairs flicked off one by one. Water ran in the maid's bath, then a door shut and all was quiet.

He was about to get up and go find a snack in the kitchen when Simone's door opened with a bang and footsteps fled down the hall toward him. He turned his head to keep his glasses from reflecting light, and froze. Simone ran right past him without a glance in his direction, took the stairs two at a time, struggled with the top half of the Dutch door in the front hall, and then flung herself up and over the bottom half, out into the night. The open half door let in a cloud of cold, moist air. A trail of beaten snow led from the hollow where she had landed, down the walk, and around the corner of the house.

Lunatic, he muttered. From the glimpse he got of her as she ran by him, he saw she was only wearing a slip. And from the sound of her argument with Violet, he knew she was no where near her right mind. Should he go after her? He could. But he was hungry. Poached eggs and hash were hardly a meal, especially after his trudge through the snow. No. He would wait. She would return, and when she did she'd need some warming up. And that was his specialty.

Once the house is raised and saddled onto the dollies, the mover builds more cribs in the yard, between the house and the truck, to support the house as it leaves its foundation. Those cribs, too, are greased with Ivory Soap.

Chapter 42

SIMONE SCRAMBLED through the top half of the Dutch door, did a clumsy somersault, and landed on her back in the mound of snow that had built up on the stone entryway during the storm. Freezing rain had laid down a sheet of ice on top of the snow, but the melt that had been underway for several hours had turned the elements into a spongy mass, a cold yet soft place for her body to fall. The heat generated by the rage of her viperous words dropped only a few degrees as she plunged out the door. She was not just an emotional hurricane; she was a volcano. Her core of lava ran deep.

She stood and brushed herself off. Her bare feet and thin ankles were cold but the night air felt warm. A mist hung over everything obscuring landmarks. She wanted to flee to the orchard, to the pear trees with their low, angular branches, but she was afraid she might lose her way so she kept close to the house. It loomed white and nearly invisible in the mist except for its dark green shutters. No lights illuminated the rooms on the front of the house and the snow drifts made it hard for her to keep her bearings. Her mind raced and jumped back and forth between her fury at Violet and her disgust with Lincoln. When she'd gone into her bathroom earlier that night to run her bath, she'd forgotten all about what she had left in the tub. When she pulled back the shower curtain, the horror of the morning's bloody sheets sent her into shock. They lay curled in a mound like a huge fetus. It might have been the mixture of wine and vodka, but she thought she saw a girl, a little dead girl, lying in the tub. She had screamed. Screamed and cursed and called up hell upon the whole house. She hated Lincoln for forcing his seed inside her night after night. It was his fault she conceived all those babies, not hers. She didn't want them, didn't want more Blankwells. And clearly her mother-in-law thought the same or why would she make Lincoln and her sleep in separate beds? Simone wasn't ready to be a mother; she was still trying to find out how to be a woman. But inside she knew the miscarriages were all her fault. You get what you wish for, her mother always said.

She had been afraid to touch the bloody sheets, so she pulled the cord for help, but when she heard feet on the stairs she remembered Violet was her enemy. She had grabbed the wretched bundle to throw at her, but the girl's presence stopped her like a wall. There was something solid in Violet that Simone could not penetrate.

But that was over. The truth had been revealed. Violet was a slut, and now Simone was dirty because she had touched that repulsive gown and seen the nakedness of that filthy black whore. She had to get the stench off her skin. She bent and scooped a handful of snow and rubbed it in her face. She took another and pressed it to her chest and down her torso, even between her legs. She rubbed more snow into her hair and dragged her fingers through its snarled mess until it stuck out from her head, making her look like a feral beast.

The snow invigorated her and she ran around the corner of the house. Light was coming from the upstairs windows, her windows. "Rapuntzel, Rapuntzel. Let down your hair," she cried. That was who she was, a trapped princess with no one to rescue her. Where was her Prince Charming? Where was her fairy godmother? Why had she let Toby go? Wasn't it his kiss that had awoken her? Lincoln's gold had turned to straw.

She went round the next corner of the house and saw a light in a downstairs window, but the shade was drawn. Violet's room. That's where all the schemes were planned— and maybe carried out. She felt sick with loathing. Simone crept forward and climbed on the thick euonymus hedge that bordered the house. The cold was gripping her now. Her teeth chattered and her feet were numb. But she was on a mission. She pressed on. Something hard and smooth was under Violet's window. She stepped down firmly and heard a crack. Suddenly her leg went through the storm window and disappeared several inches into the snow.

Her legs were so frozen she didn't feel pain, but when she reached down to touch her leg, her fingers came back sticky with blood. Her shin had a long vertical gouge. She wanted to scream, she would have screamed if she had an audience, but instead she channeled her rage into revenge. Like a wrist-slitter lounging in a tub of warm water, or a naughty little girl picking her own switch, Simone took an odd fascination in the blood spilling from her leg. She gathered a clump of the warm, thickening liquid on the end of her fingers, like a painter filling her brush, and drew on the outside of Violet's window. She painted a crude, Picasso-like nude lying, legs spread, under a tree. She reached down for more blood. *Slut*, she wrote, *You are going to Hell.* She signed the corner of the window with a five-pointed, upside-down star. The symbol of Satan.

At once her fury was spent. Her whole body was shivering and soaking wet. She made her way back to the front door, climbed inside, and went upstairs for a bath.

Chapter 43

ACROSS THE STATE AND ACROSS LAKE MICHIGAN, in another time zone and another weather pattern, Lincoln was just settling in for a second cozy night with his old friend Ginny. The two of them had been through a lot over the years: birthday parties, dancing lessons, country club picnics, fraternity bashes, even family holidays. One summer at the lake when they were young, they had lain side by side on their backs and carved their initials into the fleshy underside of a bracket fungi that grew like a low shelf off the trunk of the big oak tree on the ninth hole of the golf course. They joked how their initials—L and V—looked almost identical. Every year they returned to monitor the growth of the fungus and watched as progressively one letter tilted into the other until it looked like a single W.

"Wow," Ginny had said.

"Wedlock?" Lincoln asked.

"More like well-worn." She wasn't the romantic type; she was all business.

Lincoln and Ginny had grown up together and even had a short-lived engagement. They knew each other, body and mind. They fit together like a pair of old socks. Technically speaking they were one flesh. But Lincoln was also one flesh with Simone, as Ginny was with her affluent but boring husband. Even though Lincoln didn't hanker to the *Book of Common Prayer*, or the Bible from which it came, he couldn't escape the invisible knot that connected him to his wife. This March night when Simone lost her mind, it was his infidelities in part that spiked her hysterical cocktail. Even though she was a whole state and a Great Lake away when she screamed, a silent alarm went off in his chest just as Simone felt an invisible stab as her husband enjoyed himself in someone else's bed.

"What's wrong, Linky?" Ginny said. "Got a bout of the blues?"

"Why should I be sad?" he said. "I've got you for twelve more hours." He rolled over and slid his arm under her waist and nestled his body between her knees. She was soft and welcoming, a grandmother type of girl. Smart, no-nonsense, both feet on the ground. She was a solid Chris-Craft Runabout to Simone's sleek but tipsy day sailor. Ginny would never capsize in a storm. Her breasts were substantial and so was her inheritance. Had he made a mistake and married the wrong girl? But then he remembered: Ginny had rejected him. Oh well, he had her now, and if things went as planned, he'd be living in her neighborhood before the next snowfall. Still he couldn't throw off the uneasy feeling that nagged at his pleasure. He pushed away from her embrace and sat on the edge of the bed.

"Is it because you couldn't get through to Little Miss Muffet on the phone?" Ginny said. "Want to try again?"

"Maybe," he said, knowing it was that and much more. "But it's too late to call now and besides, the phone lines probably won't be fixed until tomorrow."

"Then come back to Mama," she said and drew open the sheets. "Sail with me to the land of Nod."

Chapter 44

RANDOLPH WAS STILL SITTING in the kitchen eating peanut butter straight from the jar and drinking hot cocoa when he heard Simone crawl back through the front door and run upstairs. She'd been outside a long time. Must be an iceberg by now. He heard water running for a bath. He'd let her soak awhile and relax before he offered his sympathies. It was just after midnight. The hour for working magic was about to begin.

A line of light shone under Violet's door. Maybe this was the time to bring out another of the tricks he had up his sleeve. He poured what remained of the hot chocolate from the saucepan into a mug and went to her door, rubbing peanut butter off his teeth with his finger.

"You awake?" he whispered. He'd take the gentle tack.

"Go away Judas."

"You have every right to be mad," he said. "I've brought you a peace offering. And I have something important to show you."

"You've caused enough trouble."

"I brought you some cocoa to help you sleep—and there's something else you need to see."

She opened the door a crack and shook her head at the mug. "Chocolate keeps me awake."

"I heard the fight upstairs. She sounded out of her mind."

"She is," Violet said. "It was awful. She was holding a mess of bloody wet sheets and saying she'd flushed her babies down the toilet. I wanted to cry."

"Down the toilet? Do you believe that? She over dramatizes everything." That was the tack he needed to take to plant more doubts in her mind. "That's just what worries me—to see her put you in so much danger."

"Danger? You think I'm in danger?"

"It's hard to tell with someone who's insane."

"You wouldn't believe the things she said to me." Violet opened the door a bit more but still didn't let him in. "She called me a whore. She thinks I seduced Mr. Lincoln, just like you said."

"You and I know that's crazy." He aligned himself with Violet. "She's completely paranoid." That was the point he needed to hammer home. "And I think I know why. Look at this." He took the purloined map from his back pocket and showed it to her.

"What is this?" She unfolded the paper.

"I found it this afternoon." He didn't mention where. "I'm almost positive it's directions to Lincoln's old girlfriend's house near Chicago. It looks like a woman's handwriting, doesn't it?"

Violet scanned the page. "Oh my God," she said. "Did you read this? *The back door will be unlocked. Or I'll meet you under the apple tree.* Signed *V.*" Her voice shook. "Simone was screaming at me about an apple tree, saying that I had seduced Lincoln under a tree."

"She just doesn't want to see the truth, does she?" He shook his head. "It's a case of mistaken identity. She wants to believe you are V."

"But I'm not. I'm not that V. It doesn't make sense."

"That's what frightens me. She doesn't make sense. She's irrational. And irrational people are dangerous." He loved the way the whole shebang was taking on a rationality of its own. It was far more ingenious than he could ever have planned.

"The last thing she said was that she would ruin me—and my family—forever."

"Oh Violet. Let's pray Lincoln comes home tomorrow and straightens the whole thing out."

"Can I keep this?" she said holding the map in her hand.

"I don't need it." Not anymore, he thought. "If I were you I'd lock my door. Just in case."

"Good night, Randolph." She shut her door and fiddled with the impotent lock to make him think it worked. When he was gone she'd push her dresser in front of the door. For now she just needed to gaze on the heavens and get some perspective. Maybe she would see a star outside her window.

When the whole contraption is in place, the mover pulls a
thick-linked cable from the cab of his truck and hooks it onto
both dollies. The truck is outfitted with a "bunk," a sixteen
foot long I-beam resting on a fifth wheel. He winches up
the chain, causing the house to slide forward on top of the
I-beams and over the slippery cribs, until it comes to rest on
the bunk, with the dollies providing stability at the sides.

Chapter 45

THE HOT CHOCOLATE WAS STILL WARM as Randolph
climbed the front stairs. He didn't want Violet to hear any
creaking outside her room. He liked this upstairs-down-
stairs, black and white adventure, as long as he had access
everywhere.

He rapped quietly on Simone's door, then pushed it
open. What squalor. Clothes strewn all over, the beds a
mess. The door to the bath was shut but that didn't deter
him. Simone was a fragile bird who needed her feathers
smoothed. He knocked once and turned the knob. A rush
of steam fogged his glasses. The air was thick with the
heady scent of jasmine.

"Don't worry," he said through the crack in the door.
"It's only me. I've brought you a cup of cocoa."

Simone sunk under the billows of bubbles covering her bath.

"Randolph, I'm exhausted. I don't have time for games."

"I know, I know," he said. "This isn't a game. This is real. I've come to bring you comfort."

"I'm in the tub," she said.

"I won't peek. In fact I'll take my glasses off. Then I'm blind as a bat. Here, take this drink before it gets cold."

"Shut the door. You're letting in a draft," she said and reached gingerly for the mug.

He entered the room, spacious for a bathroom, as big as Violet and Ambra's rooms put together. There was a chair at the foot of the tub, behind Simone's back. He sat down.

"She's gone to sleep," he said. "You don't have anything more to worry about tonight."

"I'm past worrying." She took a sip of cocoa. "Not bad, but this could use a bit of bourbon, wouldn't you say, southern boy?"

"I know something better to help you relax. A trick my mother taught me. She said I had fingers from heaven."

"From heaven? Really?" Simone placed a washcloth over her breasts. The bubbles were dispersing. "Tell me about your mother."

"Funny you ask. You remind me of her." He rolled up his sleeves, then slipped his hands into the water without touching her skin. He'd let them warm up first. "She was a real beauty, with transparent skin and amber hair. My father called her his pillar of fire." He paused. "Would you like me to rub your neck?"

She nodded.

"She was the organist at the church when my father

was hired. As far as I can tell, she *was* the church. People came from all around to hear her play." He worked the sides of her neck, then down to her shoulders. "It was a transcendentalist church so there wasn't much preaching. Much more intellectual than that. My father lectured but my mother was the spirit of the place." He made circles on the top of her breastbone.

"So that's how you learned how to play?" She handed him the empty mug and he set it on the floor.

"I watched and she taught me most of what I know." He kneaded the skin under her arms. ""You could say she inducted me into the secrets of love."

"Love?" Simone raised one leg and examined her shin. The bleeding had stopped. The warm water had soaked the cut clean. "That sounds rather risqué."

"My mother said music was the language of love." He reached down to cup her breasts. "Let me show you. I know you'll like it."

Simone lay still. This was bad, she knew, very bad. But it felt delicious. Didn't she deserve to feel good once in awhile? Hadn't she been through hell tonight? She needed a touch of heaven.

"I'll only touch you with my hands," he said. "You stay underwater. Whenever you want me to stop I will."

"You promise?" She didn't want him to stop. Lincoln had never roused these feelings in her. Only Toby.

"I promise," he said. "Let this be my gift to you. You need some relaxation, some release."

She closed her eyes and imagined that the fingers playing over her skin belonged to the handsome dark-haired boy who strummed his guitar and sang lovely melodies to her on hot summer nights. The scent of jasmine rose from the bath water. She was on the porch back home. The summer evening air carried a whisper of chill but she was warm. She was hot. She was the guitar. She was the song. She was a beautiful chord harmony. She didn't notice the bubbles growing thin. She didn't care that her body was becoming visible. She didn't even try to stifle the long glorious moan that came from the back of her throat as her hips lifted and water whooshed from the tub.

She settled back with a smile on her lips, nearly asleep. Randolph dried his hands, hooked his glasses over his ears, and slipped away without a word.

Chapter 46

VIOLET TURNED OFF HER LIGHT and raised the shade in her room. She wanted to see the wide outdoors. She wanted to think on eternity. *When I consider the heavens, the work of your fingers, the moon and the stars that you have set in place, what is man that you are mindful of him?* That was one of her mother's favorite psalms. She would recite it to them as she sat on their beds, first to the three boys laying head to toe like clothespins with two right side up and one in the middle upside down. Then she'd come over to their side of the room, hers and Rosie's, and say the same thing over again. How could she help but have it orbit, like the moon itself, around the center of her mind?

It would be good to be back home again, even with the shame of failure clinging to her like the stink of a skunk. When the dogs got into skunk, Mama rubbed them with a concoction of tomato juice and coffee and then tossed them in the river. Mama would have some recipe for cleaning this mess off her too. Violet would work hard. She'd take care of Rosie. She'd make dinner for the boys and do the laundry. Things would get better over time.

It was awfully dark out the window. She moved closer and put her nose to the pane. There was something on the glass, something smeared on it, like bird droppings or pinesap. Whatever it was, it covered the whole bottom half of her window. She sat back and stared at it, leaning from side to side. It looked like a picture, but a picture of what? All at once she saw it: a naked woman lying under a tree. And there were words, though they were backwards from the inside of the window. *Slut*, it said. *You are going to Hell.* Then in the left-hand corner, like a signature to this sinister work of art, was an upside down star.

Violet trembled and in her fury yanked at the shade. It came lose from its brackets and fell on top of her. She stood on the bed, shaking, trying to fit the ends of the shade back into the holders. She couldn't bear that abomination staring at her a moment longer.

There was no question who had done this. Simone. Wicked Simone. That girl was aligned with the devil. She was going to ruin everything Violet loved. She had already begun. Simone had lied and schemed and provoked her over and over again. Maybe she was crazy or maybe it was all an act, part of her plan to trap Violet and destroy her.

She sat on her bed, her heart thumping. Scenes from the last two days played through her mind. The watercolor Simone had painted of her beside the globe—had Simone planted that so she'd find it? What about the wine and fortune telling? Simone had invoked wicked spirits right into the house. And the eerie music she played with Randolph—were they in this together? Were the two of them lovers? Violet remembered the way they looked together opening the wine bottle in the kitchen, and later, at the top of the stairs, how Randolph had put his hands around her waist, thinking it was Simone in the kimono. Had Simone been outside with him this afternoon? Had he helped her paint the window? Was it paint—or could it be blood, blood from the dirty sheets, from the dead baby?

Violet was confused. The pieces didn't add up. What about the dressing room? Maybe Simone thought she had been seducing Randolph and was jealous?

She forced herself to sit quietly and wait. It was no good to act rashly. She steadied her breathing. Her heart slowed its pounding. She heard sounds in the house. Quiet voices upstairs. Conspiring, scheming voices. She waited a moment longer and then heard a familiar sound. The sound of sex, just like Simone made when she was with Lincoln. But this time it different; it was several notes lower as if it came straight from her belly, not her throat.

Violet was disgusted. She was repulsed. Fornication was going on right above her while she was being called a slut. This was wrong. This was indecent. This was sin. A dark curtain dropped down on the sides of her mind like blinders on a horse. All she could see was Simone. Simone flushing half-born babies down the toilet. Simone holding a knot of bloody sheets. Simone ripping her nightgown, exposing her nakedness. She heard Simone's cackling laughter, her vile curses, her pathetic whimpering, her adulterous moan. Violet hated her. Hated her with the sharp white heat of righteousness.

She turned on her light and took the Bible from the top of her pressed flowers, opening it to the book of Revelation:

Fallen, fallen is the great whore. She has become a home for demons and a haunt for every evil spirit. All the nations have drunk the wine of her adulteries. Come out of her, my people. Do not share in her sins. Give back to her as she has given; pay her back double for what she has done.

Chapter 47

VIOLET SAT WITHOUT MOVING, AS IF IN A TRANCE.

Water drained from the tub overhead. Floorboards creaked, bedsprings let out a sigh, then all was still.

More time went by.

A snore rose from Ambra's room.

Rage cooled into indignation, then mixed with fear, and began to set like cold cement turning from green to colorless grey.

The grandfather clock tolled one. Two.

The room inside Violet's mind narrowed to a pin point. There was only one way out.

Her stiff limbs ached from sitting. She shuddered with the cold that comes in the darkest hours of night when the body is meant to sleep and the mind sinks into its reptilian mode.

She stirred and stood, still clothed only in her torn gown, and walked—almost floated—to the kitchen as if in obedience to a hypnotist's command. Matches. No. Poison. No. The carving knife. She palmed the weighted handle, the blade an extension of her wrist. Mrs. B insisted all the knives be kept sharp.

She took the front stairs, retracing her path from two afternoons ago when the storm had first begun. The thick, padded carpet was soft under her bare feet. *The place on which you're standing is holy ground.*

She stood outside the door.

Remember Moses and the Egyptian.

Another voice, closer.

David and Goliath.

She put her hand on the knob and went in.

David and Uriah.

The shaft of the knife felt firm in her grip.

A man after God's own heart.

She hefted her hand, blade above her head.

A warrior princess. Protector of her tribe.

Bold in battle.

Steady in sacrifice.

Burning for righteousness.

She moved toward the bed.

The sickly smell of jasmine.

The rhythmic beat of breath.

A blood-dark pool of hair splayed against the pillow.

A pale shape floated in the pool.

A baby.

Violet stepped closer, arm curved like a scythe, eyes set hard like flint, the flint of her heart.

Simone stirred and sighed, made a sucking sound in her sleep. Her thumb was in her mouth.

Violet dropped her hand and turned away. A sob

caught in her throat. Simone was a baby, just a baby. *O God, what am I doing? Jesus, help me!*

She left the room and closed the door. She slumped at the top of the back stairs, exhausted. The damp dirty rags from this morning's cleaning were still humped in the corner where she had dropped them. A new voice spoke: *All our righteousness is as filthy rags.* As she hung her head and gazed down the stairs, a door appeared before her eyes, the door in Mama's painting back home. It was the vine-covered door with Jesus standing outside. Knocking. *Where is the handle?* she always asked Mama. *It only opens from within.*

When a house is ready to be moved, tree trimmers
have already done their work along the relocation route.
One crew from the utility company needs to take down the
power lines in front of the truck, while another reattaches
them after it passes.

Chapter 48

WARM SPRING AIR FLOWED UP THE MISSISSIPPI from
the Gulf of Mexico through New Orleans, past Missouri,
and east to the Ohio River Valley through Louisville. It
cut directly north near Cincinnati and blew into Ann
Arbor carrying traces of salt spray and sea bird voices.
It drove that northern storm east over Lake Erie to Lake
Ontario where it followed the Saint Lawrence Seaway up
past Quebec, around Newfoundland, and into the Atlantic.
As fast as the snow and rain had appeared, it disappeared.
While Violet folded her clothes and packed them into her
carpetbag and secured her collected treasures in a box, the
ice-covered snow turned to slush and then to water. What
didn't soak into the wide lawns to nourish the already waking crocus and daffodils, and set the sap flowing in the
pear trees, ran down the hill into the Huron River.

From three am until four Violet had time to do two loads of wash: Simone's sheets in one load and her uniforms in another. She wouldn't be needing those anymore. She laid out the table for breakfast and made coffee for two, for Simone and Randolph. Then she lay down on her bed, intending to rest for only a few moments, but she fell fast asleep.

Upstairs Simone tossed in her sleep. In her dream she was swimming. She was in the pool, the crystalline turquoise one at the country club down the street from her home in Louisville. Toby was with her, illegally. After his father was arrested for making moonshine, his family was blackballed. But Simone had sneaked him in and they were racing one another the length of the pool, underwater.

She stroked and kicked frog-leg style as fast as she could. Toby was half a body-length ahead of her. She was almost out of breath, straining to see the end of the pool, when the water turned dark and murky. She burst to the surface, gasping for breath. She wasn't in the pool, she was in a brackish pond, a stagnant swamp. She stood ankle deep in muck and sand. Slime-covered weeds draped from her waist. Toby, she called. Toby, where are you? From the corner of her eye she saw a shape slide into the water. She lunged fast toward the opposite bank. The water was suddenly deep, up to her waist, up to her chin. The creature—it must be a snake—slid between her legs. She shivered with horror. An awful, erotic feeling crept up her body. She awoke in a sweat.

Her head ached. She wanted to vomit. She needed a drink. No. She needed coffee. She needed fresh air. Oh

God, she needed to take a look at her life. What had happened last night? Her shoes in Violet's closet, the love letter, the bloody sheets, the fight with Violet, her crazy trip out into the snow. She must have been delirious. And Randolph. She shuddered. That was the worst of all. What was going on in this house?

She made herself sit up even though her head was pounding. Bright sun forced its way around the edge of the drapes. A bird sang. She grabbed her terry cloth robe off the floor and tied it tight around her. Her shin hurt. Had she cut herself shaving? She was confused. Her memory came in bits and pieces. There was something sinister about the bathroom adjoining her bedroom. So she went to the guest bath across the hall instead. The tile floor, cold against her bare feet, jolted her mind. Bile rose in her throat at the memory of what had gone on, of what she had allowed. *Lord, deliver me,* she cried and immediately vomited into the toilet.

After she cleaned her face and washed out her mouth she held tight to the banister and made her way down the back stairs. She would drink black coffee, put an ice bag on her head, and try to talk some sense with Violet. She wasn't sure what she'd said to the girl last night, but she knew she'd been raging. It was more than a "fit." Something had set her off and she had slipped over the edge. A person she didn't recognize had taken control. It was as if her life was a play and someone else was assigned her character.

The kitchen was empty. She poured coffee and went to Violet's room. Last night had been the first time she'd seen it. It was tiny, but pretty. Even in her furious state of mind she'd noticed some handmade cards on the dresser. She hadn't known Violet was artistic.

Ambra's door was open and that room was empty as well. Randolph must have gone to the garage. Good. Violet's door was closed. She knocked quietly.

"Violet," she whispered. "May I come in?" She must be up since the coffee was brewed.

There was no answer. She knocked harder.

"Please," she said. "It's my turn to apologize."

Violet woke to the knock. But what was she was hearing? Simone apologizing? She must be dreaming. She got up and opened the door.

"Thank you," Simone said. "May I come in?" The room was dark and the shade was pulled, but still it seemed different from last night. It looked as though Violet had packed her things. She was dressed in her own clothes, not her uniform. A carpet bag rested against the bed. Simone wished she could remember what had gone on last night. She didn't know what she'd said—or what she'd done. Had she been out in the snow? Alcohol—and rage—blanked her mind. Violet stood holding her arms, her head down. "Would you rather talk in the kitchen?"

"I'll be leaving straight away Ma'am. I don't think anything else needs to be said." Violet handed her a slip of paper from the dresser. "I've written a note for Mrs. B. I don't expect to be paid for these last two weeks. Tell her I'm sorry for everything."

"Violet, you don't look good. There's no color in your face. Come, have some coffee with me. We need to talk."

They walked to the kitchen. Simone sat down, but Violet hovered in the corner.

"Sit," Simone said.

"I can't Ma'am. You wouldn't ask me to if you knew what I'd almost done."

"I don't know what you did. I don't know what *I* did. That's why we need to talk. Please."

Violet perched on the edge of a chair on the far side of the table from Simone. "There's a lot of things you think I did that I didn't do. But there's one thing worse than all the rest that I almost did. And for that you'll always hate me."

"What could that be? You must tell me. Tell me all of it."

Violet buried her face in her hands and started to cry. "I almost killed you, Miss Simone, I almost killed you. I was crazy with rage. I took that knife and stood over your bed. I can't believe I did such a thing."

"Last night?" Simone was incredulous. "Why?"

"It was the painting on my window. You *must* have done it. And all the threats you made against me and my family. Rosie. I couldn't stand it. I lost control."

Simone knew what that was like. "What painting, what are you talking about?"

"On the window, in my room," she said, still crying. "Behind the shade by my bed."

Simone went down the hall and into Violet's room. She lifted the shade and gasped. Memory flooded back as clear and shocking as the morning sun. She had done that. With her own blood.

She went back to the kitchen where Violet waited, still as stone. "Oh God, Violet. That's terrible. What possessed me?"

"What possessed either of us?" Violet shook her head. Maybe she and Simone were more alike after all. "You thought I was sleeping with Mr. Lincoln, but it's not true.

Not the tiniest bit true." She pulled a piece of paper from her pocket. "Here, look at this. Isn't this a map to Mr. Lincoln's friend's house?"

"Ginny's?" Simone sat down and smoothed the folded page on the table. "I think you're right," she said, reading the directions. "And what's this at the bottom? A message from V?"

"It's not me, Miss Simone. I swear…."

Simone cut in. "This handwriting is familiar. I've seen something else written by this person." She reached in the pocket of her robe. The love letter was still there. She put it on the table next to the map. "See the V?" she said. "It's the same. Oh my God, Ginny's real name is Virginia!"

Violet read the letter. "I know what this is," she said. "It's from the Bible—the Song of Songs."

"What?" Simone looked puzzled.

"It's a love poem, part of the Bible. She must have copied it out nearly word for word, just getting rid of the old fashioned language."

"That woman isn't creative enough to write her own love letter—she has to use the Bible to seduce my husband!" Simone laughed in scorn. "But this—it's practically proof of adultery." As she said those last words, an image flashed through her mind, of herself in the bathtub, with Randolph bent over the side. Shame and disgust flooded her soul. Her marriage was a sham.

"Where did you find this?" Violet said. She looked softly at Simone, willing her to calm down.

"My mind is confused. It's hard to remember, though it had something to do with…" She couldn't say his name.

"I know—it was in my shoe, my pink slipper that was in your closet."

"My closet? I didn't take your shoe. And I've never seen that letter before."

"Where did you find that map?"

"I didn't find it. Randolph gave it to me."

"He gave me the slippers from your closet."

"Randolph told me you were crazy and that I was in danger from you."

"That's what he told me about you."

They looked at each other across the table.

Chapter 49

THERE WERE ENOUGH PATCHES OF SNOW left on the ground for Violet and Simone to see that Randolph had backed his truck out of the garage and driven down the drive. They picked their way through puddles and slush until they came to the stairs at the far end of the garage. Simone insisted on bringing the big cast iron skillet just in case, though Violet knew he would be gone.

When they got to the top of the stairs, the door was off its hinges. The rooms were a shambles. The table upturned. The two wooden chairs smashed and broken on the floor. The upholstery on the love seat had been slashed; so had the mattress in the bedroom. Broken glass from the mirror filled the sink and reflected jagged images off the walls. The appliquéd bedspread, one of Mrs. B's creations, was partially stuffed into the wood-burning stove. Luckily the bulky fabric had smothered the fire or the whole place would have burned. Worst of all was the piano, the old Baldwin in the corner. The ax from the woodshed stuck straight out of the shattered case. Most of the keys had been chopped off—both black and white—and were missing.

They looked at each other, speechless.

Violet took the frying pan from Simone's hand. She knew how heavy it was.

"We can clean this up later, she said. " Let's go have breakfast."

At the new home site, the mover reverses the process and slides the house onto its new foundation, bolting it onto the concrete blocks. Of course a house cut in two requires much patching and repairing, with new walls and windows filling the scar where the other half had been. But with careful workmanship and imagination, the two new houses can become neighbors, and even friends.

Chapter 50

THE OUTRAGE CAUSED BY RANDOLPH'S ACTIONS sent Mr. and Mrs. Blankwell and their son Lincoln into a fury. Lincoln's indignation, however, was waylaid when Simone presented him with the letter and the map. He had his hands full trying to placate his wife.

Mrs. Blankwell called in the chief of police and two private investigators who never found a trace of Randolph. The handyman scandal soon faded in importance when the *Michigan Daily* arrived at the doorstep with a headline announcing the new Veteran's Hospital and the government's right of eminent domain.

Simone begged Violet to stay, saying she needed her, until Violet promised not to leave. Violet listened to stories of Toby. Simone cried when she heard about Earl. When the weather was nice they went for walks, and on rainy days, they thumbed through books on art. Simone avoided the piano and Violet made sure she had plenty of tea to drink on long afternoons.

After angry phone calls and legal threats failed to halt the United States government, the house was divided into three pieces and moved down the street. The two smaller, more manageable homes are still neighbors on Cedar Bend Drive today. The remains of the two-story garage cannot be found.